Joey and Dawson stood close together. He was still holding her hand.

What are we now, Dawson? Joey wondered, her eyes searching his. *What will happen when we all go away to college? How am I supposed to get through each day without seeing your face?*

"What are you thinking?" Dawson asked, his voice low.

"Nothing much." She edged away from him, and he dropped her hand. "You know, you're right, Dawson. Frankly, my own seriousness is boring me to tears. Let's just for once be young and crazy and not think everything to death. Agreed?"

"Agreed."

"Darling Capesiders!" Muffy Smitham called expansively. "It's time. Let the Capeside Winter Follies Auditions begin!"

Dawson's Creek™

A Capeside Christmas

Based on the television series "Dawson's Creek"™
created by **Kevin Williamson**

Written by C. J. Anders

First published 2000 by Pocket Pulse
Pocket Books, a division of Simon & Schuster, Inc.
1230 Avenue of the Americas, New York, NY 10020

This edition published 2001 by Channel 4 Books
an imprint of Macmillan Publishers Ltd
20 New Wharf Road, London N1 9RR
Basingstoke and Oxford

Associated companies throughout the world
www.panmacmillan.com

ISBN 0 7522 1985 5

9 8 7 6 5 4 3 2 1

A CIP catalogue record for this book is available from
the British Library.

Printed and bound in Great Britain by Mackays of Chatham plc

For Ashley and Shannon

A Capeside Christmas

Chapter 1

Joey Potter squinted into the bright afternoon sun as she and her friend Pacey Witter headed for the high school. A gust of wind made her zip her parka up to her neck. The forecast had called for snow the next day, but so far there were no signs of it. Still, you could tell it was December—it was really, really cold.

She and Pacey Witter walked into the noisy school auditorium. It was already packed with people of all ages. The walls were festooned with holly wreaths, and a large Christmas tree decorated with home-made ornaments sat majestically on the stage. Next to the tree, a pianist was banging out Christmas carols on an old upright piano, urging people to sing along.

"Well, how very festive," Pacey remarked.

"Deck the halls, fa-la-la-la-la, et cetera, et cetera," Joey replied with a noticeable lack of enthusiasm. "Merry Christmas and all that."

At the end of one aisle, Sandi Rudman, who had graduated from Capeside High a year ago and was now a freshman at the Tisch School of Drama at New York University, stood with a clipboard under a giant sign that read CAPESIDE WINTER FOLLIES: AUDITIONS SIGN UP HERE. A line of people waiting to sign up to audition snaked all the way to the back of the theater.

Joey turned to Pacey. "Remind me again why we're doing this."

"Tradition, Potter, tradition. We live in Capeside. Capeside goes nuts every year for the Capeside Winter Follies. Ergo, we who live here go nuts, too—"

"And yet we've managed to survive in this town for sixteen years observing Capeside Winter Follies from afar, albeit with a slightly superior half-smile curling our adolescent lips," Joey reminded him. "I see no need to break a winning record now. A couple more years of high school, and we can escape unscathed by—"

"Potter, Potter, Potter," Pacey chided her. "Where's that small-town Christmas spirit? *It's a Wonderful Life* and all that? You know, I heard our pastoral village was the location that Frank Capra really wanted."

"You can find my small-town spirit in George Bailey's bank, along with my small-town savings account—so small that even if the bank failed, it would hardly make a difference," Joey retorted. "Now, I figure that if I wait tables at Leery's restaurant over the holiday break, I can make—"

"Hey, guys," Jen Lindley called. As she walked over to them, she had to dodge a little girl practicing her baton twirling. "What a scene, huh?"

Pacey clasped his hands to his chest. "A scene that warms the cockles of my heart. What is a cockle, by the by?"

"I'll go look it up for you," Joey offered. "Then, I'll stroll over to the restaurant and announce that I am going to work double shifts for the next two weeks whether they need me or not."

"Hey, all four of us agreed that we'd be in the Follies this year," Jen reminded her. "Right after Thanksgiving. I was there, I saw it and heard it with my own eyes and ears. So there's no backing out now."

"Not even if I plead temporary insanity due to a turkey-induced L-tryptophan overdose?" Joey asked.

"Not even. Anyone seen Dawson?" Jen craned her neck around, trying to spot him in the crowded auditorium. "We need to practice our number."

Joey stared at Jen. "Your number? How did you get Dawson Leery, also known as The Man Who Remains Behind the Camera at All Times, to agree to *sing* with you? In *public*? In the *Follies*?"

"It must have been my *femme fatale* charm," Jen replied.

Joey laughed.

"Oh, there's Dawson," Jen said. "Over by what's-her-name. The Follies stage manager."

3

"Sandi Rudman," Joey filled in. "She was two years ahead of us."

"Un-uh, haven't you heard?" Pacey asked. "No longer Sandi anyone. She went and changed her name."

"To what?" Jen asked.

Pacey grimaced. "Sundae Ramone. You know, for her major motion picture career."

Joey eyed him dubiously. "Sundae Ramone? I really hope you're kidding."

"Alas, I'm not. One lead in Capeside High's production of *Oklahoma* and the girl goes off to conquer the wonderful and wacky world of show business. I guess she thought Sandi didn't sound show-bizzy enough."

"Might I remind you that she sucked royally in *Oklahoma?*" Joey said. "Even by small-town standards? It's a good thing her parents could afford to send her to New York to school." She pushed a stray strand of her long brown hair behind one ear.

"Maybe she improved," Pacey ventured.

"Doubtful," Joey replied, as Jen eyed Sundae contemplatively. The stage manager was signing a few other potential cast members.

"She does have sort of an Ally McBeal thing going on," Jen noticed. "We have to audition for her?"

"And Muffy," Pacey said.

"Muffy?" Jen echoed. "Muffy who?"

"If memory serves, Lindley, you moved here from New York City a few years ago. Which makes you at least an honorary Capesider. How can you not know

4

about Capeside's very own diva of the Winter Follies, the incomparable Muffy Smitham?"

"Mental block. There were way too many Muffies at the boarding school I used to attend." Jen made a face. "It's such a not-cute name."

"Well, our own little Muffy is quite the hottie," Pacey pronounced, straight-faced. "Think Joan Crawford in a platinum blond wig, circa *Mommy Dearest*. Only older. Much older. And when peeved, not quite as pleasant."

"Scary." Jen shuddered.

"Beyond," Joey agreed. At that moment, a large woman strode onto the stage. She wore a massive fur coat of some sort, dyed cobalt blue, and matching thigh-high blue boots, and her thick blond hair fell rakishly over one eye.

"Okay, people, people, lovely people!" she called expansively, throwing her arms out wide. "How I adore returning to my humble beginnings each year!"

"Enter, stage left," Joey muttered. "Muffy Smitham, right on cue."

"My darlings," the woman called out to the room in general. "Every time I see you all again, I think 'Muffy, it truly is a wonderful life!'" There was a smattering of sycophantic applause.

"Does she provide barf bags with that line?" Jen asked.

"This is only the beginning," Pacey reminded her. "Did the betting pool start yet?"

"I haven't made an up-close-and-personal assessment," Joey said, tapping her chin. "However, even from this distance, I feel fairly certain."

She pulled a dollar from the back pocket of her jeans. "I say eyes. Definitely eyes."

Jen looked bewildered. "What are you two talking about?"

"Eyes, huh?" Pacey mused, ignoring Jen. He studied Muffy, who was deep in conversation with Capeside's mayor. "I beg to differ. I'm calling neck. In fact, I'm sure it's neck. Note the noticeable lack of wattle. I'm in. Say for three bucks. No. Make it five."

"Do you mind letting me in on the subject of this conversation?" Jen asked.

"Cosmetic enhancement," Pacey explained. "Better known as plastic surgery."

"Muffy 'fixes' something pretty much every year," Joey explained to Jen. "Even those of us who have abstained from participating in the Follies get in on the betting. Last year the winner took home more than two hundred dollars."

"The woman has had more plastic surgery than Michael Jackson," Pacey told Jen. "She's been lifted and tucked so many times I'm surprised she doesn't have eyes in the back of her head."

Jen laughed. "That's funny."

Pacey offered a lavish bow and looked at Joey. "You see, Potter, I'm funny. You can't lose with a partner like me. Especially if I win the betting pool."

Bill Curtson, a short, muscular guy they knew from school, strode over to them. He pulled a small notebook from his back pocket. "Bets, people?"

Pacey nodded and handed him six dollars. "I'm in for five on the neck. Potter's in for a buck; she's calling it eyes."

A Capeside Christmas

Bill scribbled something in the notebook. "So far the line is eyes, two to one. You in, Jen? Thighs are still up for grabs."

"I'll pass."

Bill nodded and stuck the notebook into his back pocket. "I'll keep you posted. We should have a winner by the end of the week." He hurried off.

"How long has this betting on Muffy's plastic surgery been going on?" Jen asked.

"Since before your time," Joey replied. It came out nastier than she had intended it.

"Since before Jesus' time," Pacey said. "The woman's gotta be a hundred and fifty years old or something. Last year Emily LaPaz won big on hips lipo."

Jen laughed. "Now, how could Emily possibly know that Muffy had lipo on her thighs?"

"Locker room, The Fitness Center," Joey said. "Nudity knows no secrets. Besides, Muffy loves to brag about her latest 'enhancement.' She considers them a badge of honor and of affluence."

Jen shook her head. "All this in Capeside?"

Joey shrugged. "Contrary to what you might think, Jen, things *do* happen in our little burg."

Jen looked at her strangely. "Are you mad at me or something?"

Joey shrugged noncommittally. "I was just answering your question."

"No, what you were and are doing is taking snide little swipes at me," Jen insisted. "So I'd like to know what precipitated them."

Joey felt her face flush. Jen was right. She had

been nasty. And for no good reason, either. The crazy thing was, she actually liked Jen most of the time. So then, why did Jen bring out the worst in her? Maybe because Jen was a curvy, self-confident, sophisticated rich blonde from New York—everything that Joey was not. And it irked Joey that after all this time, she still couldn't stop comparing herself to Jen.

It was so juvenile, reeking of pathetic insecurity. True, Joey had spent years being known to the entire town of Capeside as the motherless-girl-from-the-wrong-side-of-the-tracks-whose-dad-is-in-prison, but she'd always held her head high and never let any of the town gossips show they could get to her. Mostly, they didn't anymore.

But Jen did. And Jen never seemed to try to get to her. Which somehow made the whole thing worse.

"Look, you should definitely ignore me," Joey told her. "Nerves bring out the witch in me sometimes. I still can't believe I agreed to audition with Pacey."

"Attention please, dear people!" Muffy called from the stage. She'd made her way downstage practically to the footlights. "Make sure you sign in with my right arm and leg, the divine Miss Sundae." She gestured theatrically toward the stage manager, who shook her curls off her face in acknowledgment. "We'll get started shortly."

"Hey, what's up?" Dawson asked, as he hurried over to them. "Zoo in here, huh?"

"It's not the visitors, it's the zookeeper and her right arm and leg who concern me," Jen said, as she watched Muffy air-kiss various people onstage. "How old is that woman?"

"Muffy hasn't shared that particular data with me," Dawson said. "However, according to my parents, she's directed the Follies since sometime during the Vietnam war, and she was old then. You do the math."

"How very Dorian Gray," Jen mused, as up onstage, she watched Muffy swish her platinum blond hair around like a second-string, tenth-grade cheerleader.

"I was thinking, Dawson," Joey began, "your parents must need extra help for the holiday season, and I certainly don't mind simply being in the audience for the Follies, cheering all of you on. So, I thought I could waitress, maybe hostess, and—"

"I'm sure if you want a few hours, maybe they could work something out," Dawson said. "But they've already hired some college kids home on break. And you know that once you're cast in the Follies, Muffy demands a stringent rehearsal schedule."

"Gee, too bad I have to miss all that." Joey began to back away. "But economics trumps art. So, listen, I know the three of you are going to be fantastic up there. I'll just be going—" She collided with something and swung around.

Correction. Someone. Gale Leery, Dawson's mom.

"Oops. Sorry, Mrs. Leery," Joey told her.

"You never know who you're going to bump into." Gale gave Joey a quick hug. "Wow, big turnout, huh?"

"You know, Mrs. Leery, I was just on my way over to the restaurant," Joey told her. "Dawson mentioned that you might need extra help and I've got free time for the next two weeks, so I thought—"

"Sure, if you want to put in a few hours, we'll find you a shift or two," Gale agreed. "If you can fit it in around rehearsals."

"I think the theater can do without me," Joey said. "Actually, I feel certain that the whole show will be better off without me."

Pacey stepped in between Gale and Joey. "Mrs. Leery, don't fall for her artifice. No way you're getting out of this, Potter," he insisted. "One for all and all for one. A deal's a deal, no backing out, because—my God, what is McPhee *holding*?"

They all turned around to see their friend—and Pacey's former girlfriend—Andie McPhee, standing near the stage. She was talking with her brother Jack, and had something humanoid cradled in her arms.

"Unless she's been hiding something from us for the past nine months, I'd say it looks like a wooden doll," Jen said. "Dressed, that is."

"Yes, it certainly does," Pacey agreed. "And my next query would be: Why is Andie holding a wooden doll dressed like a human being?"

"Childhood flashback?" Joey guessed.

"Regression therapy?" Dawson guessed.

Jen grinned at them. "Wrong."

"Meaning that you know what she's up to?" Joey asked.

Jen nodded. "It seems that once upon a time Andie studied ventriloquism."

Pacey's jaw fell open. "You're telling me that my ex, the former love of my life, the girl I know everything about, has a secret and tawdry past with a dummy?"

"We try not to refer to you that way," Jen said sweetly. She turned to Gale. "So, I'm taking it as a good sign that you're here. Are you and Mitch going to sing with us after all?"

Sing with them? Joey thought, feeling left out all over again.

"Put me in the undecided column," Gale said. "I just ducked my head in here to get the first whiff of Christmas. When Muffy Smitham arrives to hold auditions, I know it means the holiday season is really beginning. See you later at home, Dawson."

She hugged her son, and then waved to some friends as she left.

"Your mom and dad are going to sing with you and Jen?" Joey asked, trying to sound casual.

Dawson shrugged. "It's a big maybe right now. My powers of persuasion have thus far been met with ambivalent indecision," he admitted. "I thought it might be good for us, as a family. But frankly, I think Jen is a better negotiator than I'll ever be."

"Hey, I'm going to sign us up to audition," Pacey told Joey. "Back in a flash."

He headed for the line before she could stop him, and Jen excused herself to the ladies' room, which left Joey standing alone with Dawson.

"This is going to be a monumentally fun experience, you'll see," Dawson promised, leaning against the wall. "So, what are you and Pacey doing for the Follies?"

"Not singing."

"I had already eliminated that possibility," Dawson said. "We have enough would-be Tony Bennetts. Then what?"

"I don't want to talk about it. Ask Pacey. But just out of curiosity, Dawson, since when is singing on your list of talents?"

"Not counting a certain inebriated rendition of some blues classic I performed on my sixteenth birthday or our early Karaoke versions of 'Daydream Believer', it pretty much isn't."

"So then, you're planning to humiliate yourself in song because—?"

"Because it's my only shot at getting Gale and Mitch to join in the Follies," Dawson admitted. "And this season, I want us all to be in it together. We don't have that many Christmases left before I graduate. Okay, it was Jen's idea. You know they both love to sing. But no way were either of them going to come up with the idea of singing in the Follies."

"I'm not tracking, Dawson."

"Jen thought that if we asked them to sing with us and explained to them that we had to have a lead and three backups—"

"They couldn't turn you down," Joey filled in. "Gee, that Jen Lindley. Always thinking."

Dawson studied her closely for a moment. "Did I miss something?"

"What?"

"Because you sound mad, Joe."

"I'll have to work on that, then, won't I?"

"Seriously, Joey. What's up?"

He took her hand and held it; the concern on his face made Joey feel ashamed of her own pettiness.

"Forget it, Dawson. I'm just channeling Scrooge, or something. And I'm also ruing the day I agreed to do a comedy routine with Pacey."

"Comedy?" Dawson looked dubious.

"You got it. Pacey said he'd write it if I would just be up there with him."

Dawson smiled. "You know, you'll be great. Besides, if you don't do it, you'll look back and regret that you didn't join in. College looms. Nothing stays the same. We have to enjoy the moment while we're in it."

"And that's why you want to be in the Follies this year? Out of some misplaced sense of nostalgia for your Capeside youth, a youth that isn't even over?"

"But it will be. Sometimes it seems as if I can actually feel it slipping out of my grasp."

They stood close together. He was still holding her hand.

What are we now, Dawson? Joey wondered, her eyes searching his. *What will happen when we all go away to college? How am I supposed to get through each day without seeing your face?*

"What are you thinking?" Dawson asked, his voice low.

"Nothing much." She edged away from him, and he dropped her hand. "You know, you're right, Dawson. Frankly, my own seriousness is boring me to tears. Let's just for once be young and crazy and not think everything to death. Agreed?"

"Agreed."

"Darling Capesiders!" Muffy called expansively. "It's time. Let the Capeside Winter Follies Auditions begin!"

Chapter 2

"Where the heck is everyone?" Andie groused to Jen, checking her watch. "Rehearsal starts in five minutes."

"If they chicken out, they die," Jen promised.

"Chickening out is not Pacey Witter's style."

"Not Dawson's, either," Jen agreed. "Or Joey's, for that matter." She stomped her feet to try to warm them up.

They were hanging around the entrance to the high school, as was most of the cast of the Follies. It was nearly seven o'clock, the sun had set hours earlier, and it was seriously cold out. However, standing outside in the freezing cold was still better than being inside. The heat in the auditorium was acting up, and the temperature was a few degrees above intolerable.

It was the first rehearsal of Capeside Follies. Auditions had gone reasonably smoothly the evening before, even though Muffy and Sundae had conducted them as if for a Broadway opening instead of for a community theater revue that had been performed, with minor variations, dozens of times before.

Amazingly, Joey and Pacey's Abbott and Costello-based comedy routine had been accepted into the show. It was slotted for the first act, along with Jen and Dawson's song. As for Gale and Mitch singing backup, they'd been unable to attend the auditions, but had sent word to Muffy that, schedule at the restaurant permitting, they were in.

"Yo, Andie McPhee, you in on the Muffy betting pool?" Bill Curtson asked, sidling over to Andie. "We're in the last hour of taking bets."

"Gambling isn't in my nature, Bill, but thanks for asking."

He nodded, apparently trying to think of something else to say. It made Jen smile. It was so obvious that he had a crush on Andie, and that Andie was oblivious to it.

"So, what are you doing over winter vacation?" Bill finally asked Andie.

She gave him a curious look. "Gee, Bill. The Follies."

He laughed self-consciously. "Right, just a joke. So, wow, it's like a major torrid zone in the auditorium."

"We know, Bill," Andie said. "That's why we're out here freezing our butts off."

"Right! Knew that! So, catch you later, okay?" Bill took off.

"He's got a thing for you," Jen announced.

"Please."

"He does," Jen insisted. "I have radar for these things. Notice how even out here on the frozen tundra he was sweating at your very nearness."

"Maybe he has a thyroid problem. Ah, the icemen cometh." Andie cocked her head at Dawson and Pacey, who were hurrying toward them.

Jen squinted in their direction. "What're they carrying?" As the two guys drew closer, they could see that Pacey and Dawson were lugging huge cartons in their arms.

"Please tell me there's an air conditioner in there, because the auditorium is having a hot flash," Jen begged.

"Better," Pacey pronounced. "So certain am I of winning the Muffy betting pool, that I have made the premature but grand gesture of purchasing Krispy Kremes for the masses."

"I love a man who gambles on his gambles," Jen quipped, "especially when it involves massive amounts of sugar for us all."

"It's just the kind of loyal team player I am," Pacey replied, as he and Dawson set the trays of doughnuts down on one of the steps. "Hey, hey, hey!" Pacey called through cupped hands. "The sugar shock's on me, come and get 'em!"

The trays were immediately surrounded by dozens of hungry Follies cast members, and doughnuts began to disappear. Just then Muffy stuck her head out the backstage door to the auditorium and took in the wild scene.

"Pacey Witter brought everyone doughnuts!" Serena Rudman, Sundae's little sister, sang out, her mouth full of jelly doughnut. Serena was only eight, but she'd been picked by Muffy to sing the song "Happiness" from *You're a Good Man, Charlie Brown* to open the second act of the show, which segued into "We Love You, Capeside" to the tune of "We Love You, Conrad" from *Bye, Bye, Birdie*. Serena and Sundae's mother, Sage, hovered over her daughter, certain that Serena was a star in the making.

Muffy applauded and beamed at Pacey. "That is so thoughtful of you, darling. Real cast spirit. I'll remember that."

"Thank you, ma'am," Pacey replied gravely. "That means a lot, coming from you. I just have to say, this moment wouldn't be happening without you."

Jen snorted a laugh through her doughnut.

"You're too, too kind, darling," Muffy said, beaming.

"If I'm not being too bold, might I add that I've been admiring your swanlike neck," Pacey continued. "It looks so very youthful."

"Funny," Bill Curtson put in, "I was just thinking that about your eyes, ma'am," he prompted.

Everyone waited. Would Muffy make her plastic surgery confession this early?

"Aren't you both darling," Muffy purred. "All right, people, time to get started. True art waits for no man or woman." She disappeared back inside the stage door.

"Thus, the betting pool continues," Pacey said, sighing, as he reached for the last doughnut on the tray.

Back in Capeside, back in Capeside
Back in Capeside by the sea
I'm so glad to be in Capeside
Home for Christmas, you and me.

The entire Follies cast was assembled onstage, singing to the tune of "Clementine." It was a Follies tradition that allegedly went back to the very first Follies, many decades ago, that the first act would end with the Capeside version of "Clementine."

"That's it, everyone, sing out!" Muffy bellowed, over Chester Pinkley's energetic pounding on the slightly out-of-tune piano.

Capeside's festive, and so restive
For our friends and company
How we love to come to Capeside
Lovely Capeside by the sea.

In the back row, Joey wiped a bead of perspiration from her forehead with the back of her hand and made a face at the photocopied lyrics in her hand. "These lyrics may be a new low in the art form," she mumbled to Jen. "Who wrote this? Doesn't Muffy know that restive means ill-at-ease?"

"I asked Dawson the same thing. No one seems to remember anymore. He says the word 'restive' was in the lyrics at the first show, and it stuck."

"Isn't it about time that somebody put it out of its misery?"

"Great idea. You be the one to tell Muffy," Jen suggested.

"Final verse, darlings!" Muffy called. "Sing it like you mean it, from the heart. Use the heat, people, let it warm your spirits as you sing!"

I love Capeside, I love Capeside
I love Capeside by the sea.
Christmas spirit, brings me near it
Back to Capeside, by the seeeea.

"Bravo!" Muffy clapped her hands, as the cast stood around uncertainly. "Bravo! That was excellent for our first rehearsal." She nodded at Sundae, who stood by her side.

"Fifteen, people, fifteen-minute break!" Sundae called. "Get some water and cool down."

"And then we'll work on the grand finale, darlings," Muffy promised. "I've got something wonderful worked up for this year."

The cast bolted toward the water fountain in the hallway or toward the stage door for some fresh air. Sundae and an aged custodian tried to get the windows open, but it was hopeless.

Pacey stepped out the stage door, ski parka in hand. "Nature's deodorant," he told the cast. "Everyone, lift your arms!"

"I find myself wishing we already had snow," Dawson told him. "I can imagine myself rolling around in it right about now."

"Dawson?"

Dawson turned around. Sundae Ramone was next to him. Her brown curls fell into her eyes in a way that seemed obvious and planned for a fetching effect. She wore baggy jeans and an oversize sweater that enhanced her ragamuffin look. She was so slender she looked as if she hadn't eaten a decent meal since last Christmas.

"Hi, Sand—er, Sundae," Dawson said. He slipped his jacket on but didn't zip it up.

"With whipped cream and a cherry on top," Sundae quipped, waiting for Dawson to chuckle.

He didn't.

"So, wow, being back here seems unreal, you know?" she continued. "I mean, after being in New York and everything? Capeside is, like, so tiny and provincial."

"I prefer to think of it as homey and quaint, actually," Dawson said.

"Whatever. You can't wait to escape, right?"

Dawson shrugged. "Some days yes, some days no."

She rubbed her skinny arms for warmth. "So, ask me how school is."

"How's school?"

"Awesome, seriously. N.Y.U. is just so incredible. I'm learning to really get in touch with myself, to access my deepest emotions so that I can, like, inhabit my characters." She stuck her hands under her armpits. "So, I seem to recall that you're interested in film?"

"More like passionate about it," Dawson said.

She shook her curls out of her eyes and gave him a dimpled smile. "Passion is good. I've been exploring passion myself."

Dawson nodded. He found himself with absolutely nothing to say to her, which for him was unusual. She just seemed to be utterly calculating and disingenuous, though he couldn't figure out quite why he felt that way.

From over Sundae's shoulder, Pacey wriggled his eyebrows at Dawson and gave Sundae a significant look, which clearly meant that he thought Sundae was into Dawson. Dawson tried hard to ignore him.

"I've really been getting into performance art," Sundae went on. "Have you explored that?"

" 'Performance art' is one of those terms that makes me highly suspicious," Dawson replied. "I mean, what does it mean, really?"

"Honesty, bravery, like that. Okay, take Karen Finley. I'm sure you've heard of her because she's like the most famous performance artist in the world. I saw her do a piece where she undressed while she recited names from the Manhattan White Pages at random, while smearing chocolate pudding all over herself."

"I'm sorry, Sundae, but I really don't get it."

"Wow, you're serious? 'Cause I got it. She's expressing the innate sameness of all people. Now, at the end of her performance, she rolls around in mud, then in blood, then in mashed bananas."

"You're kidding."

"That's what I heard, anyway. To represent the various colors of people," Sundae explained. "Like mud is brown, so—"

"That part I get."

"She's like my idol. So listen, if you're ever in the city, you should check out my performance art piece. I'm doing it every Monday night at this artist's loft in SoHo. He's a sculptor. I run naked around his work expressing it. Physically."

"Uh huh." Dawson checked his watch. Five more minutes of break time left. Maybe he could think of a way to politely excuse himself—

"So, how often do you get to the city, anyway?" Suddenly, Sundae was so close he could examine the pores on her face. Not that he particularly wanted to.

"Not very often."

"Because I was just thinking. If you ever need a place to crash when you're there, we could hook up."

The idea held for Dawson the appeal of hooking up with, say, Muffy. "Thanks for the offer, Sundae, but—"

"Oh wow, I just got the greatest idea. You could like crash at my place for a long weekend and you could video my performance piece."

Aha, Dawson thought. *Her ulterior motive finally rears its ugly little head.*

"We're in intersession now," Sundae continued, "and I'm supposed to get a video of my piece for my intersession project." She hooked an arm through his. "I could make it worth your while."

Dawson stepped smoothly away from her. "Sorry,

Sundae, but I'll be tied up with the Follies for the next couple of weeks. And so will you, for that matter."

"We could sneak back to the city for like just one Monday night," she wheedled. "I'll let you keep a copy of the video. You can use it when you apply to colleges. They love stuff like that. No one wants to read application essays, anyway."

"Excuse me, Sandi, but according to my watch our break is over," Serena said, striding over to them. "It's not running fast, either. I checked."

"It's Sundae and I'm on top of it," Sundae said through clenched teeth. She leaned over and whispered into Dawson's ear. "We'll talk later. Mmmm, you smell good enough to eat."

"Hey, it's snowing!" Andie cried from behind Dawson, giving her brother Jack an exuberant hug. "This is so great!"

Dawson turned his face to the sky. Sure enough, large flakes landed on his eyelashes; others swirled around him toward the ground.

"Maybe we'll get snowed in with Muffy," Jack cracked.

"Muffy with the line-free and oh-so-youthful neck," Pacey added. After that, Sundae yelled out that it was time to get back to work and led the way back into rehearsal.

"Making a new friend?" Joey asked, falling in beside Dawson.

"Perish the thought," he replied.

"She seems quite taken with you, Dawson. You could do worse. After all, she's an older woman, a drama major at N.Y.U., cute in an anorexic sort of way—"

"I have zero interest in her, Joey."

"Everyone onstage, darling people," Muffy called to them.

Joey and Dawson followed her directions. "Be that as it may, Dawson," Joey continued, "she definitely and obviously has a great deal of interest in you. And I have to say, she doesn't look like the type of girl who takes no for an answer."

Five hours later, Dawson was in bed but he was too excited to sleep. He knew he was being child-ish—no, worse than that, infantile. But ever since he could remember, the first snowstorm of the year filled him with so much happiness that sleep was impossible.

Sometimes, Capeside got really huge blizzards, when nor'easter storms rolled up the eastern seaboard and stalled off Cape Cod. Though the salt air from the ocean tended to melt accumulated snow very quickly, there were some days when there'd be so much snow on the ground that the Capeside Volunteer Fire Department had to mark the fire hydrants with long poles stuck in the ground.

This wasn't going to be one of those storms—the forecast called for no more than six inches of snow. But still . . .

Dawson got up and padded to his window, press-ing his face against the cold glass and looking out at the lone light down by the dock. Just as he had a hundred times as a kid, he peered closely at that light, trying to see if snow was still falling. It was. Not as heavily as an hour before, but it was still coming down. And there had to be close to six inches on the ground already.

That was it. The decision was made before he could think about it. "I'm sixteen years old, I'm losing my mind," he said to himself. But still, he went to his closet, pulled on some jeans and a shirt, and found his down vest and old work gloves on the floor. He didn't bother with a winter hat—just an old baseball cap. Then, silently, he made his way downstairs and into the garage.

There it was, hanging on the wall as it always did.

The Flexible Flyer sled had once belonged to his father. Mitch had kept it in pristine condition all these years, sharpening and waxing the blades, varnishing the wood, lubricating the steering mechanism.

Dawson took it down off the wall. "Rosebud," he said, smiling. He'd named his sled that after having seen the classic movie *Citizen Kane*. He took Rosebud and clomped around to the backyard. The snow packed easily under his feet, wet and heavy—perfect for sledding.

Without a moment's hesitation, he took three running steps down the gentle slope that led to the inlet they called the creek, jumped onto Rosebud, and rode it to the bottom. He came to a gentle stop fifteen feet from the dock, directly under the light that he could see from his bedroom window.

He lay prone on the sled for a long moment, savoring the silence that only snow can bring, then packed a snowball in his hands and flung it out into the middle of the creek. It splashed with an audible *ker-chunk*.

From across the water: "Nice shot, Dawson! You trying to snowball bomb some poor fish into fish food?"

He almost laughed out loud. He'd recognize that voice anywhere. Dawson peered across the creek. There, in a summer lawn chair on her own dock, under her own light, sat Joey, snow falling around her.

Somehow, that was just perfect.

Wordlessly, he climbed into the skiff that was kept tied up at the dock even in wintertime and rowed across the creek, the snowflakes lapping gently at his exposed neck. It only took a minute to get across to Joey's dock and to throw a line for Joey to tie on one of the pilings. A moment later, they were standing together.

Joey had a snowflake caught in her eyebrow. Dawson thought he'd never seen anything more beautiful.

"Some things don't change, Dawson," Joey said softly. "You're always a sucker for the first snow."

"Oh, and you aren't? Who was sunbathing in the mini-blizzard just now?"

She smiled her acknowledgment. "Got any sled tracks on your lawn yet?"

"I was trying to restrain myself. Like a mature person."

"Forget maturity, Dawson," Joey replied. "It's highly overrated. Especially during the first snow.

What I want to know is, why isn't everyone outside now? Can you just tell me why?"

"No. But I can tell you this, Joey. I'm glad they're not."

The two of them stood together on the dock in perfect silence, and let it snow.

Chapter 3

"What do you mean, Muffy has *left the show*?" Sage Rudman sputtered, as soon as the mayor of Capeside made his announcement. "What's going to happen to my daughters, Mr. Mayor? They've counted on this experience."

It was the following evening. The cast, crew, and parents of the kids involved in the Follies had been gathered together in the auditorium for a hastily called emergency meeting an hour before the regularly scheduled rehearsal. The heater was no longer on overdrive; instead, it seemed to have broken completely. People could see their breath when they spoke, and everyone wore their coats and hats for warmth.

The mayor looked crestfallen. "As I said, I sincerely apologize, it was totally unexpected. But Muffy

Smitham sent a fax to my office this morning explaining that she had received a more lucrative offer from the town of Teaneck, New Jersey, to direct its Christmas/Chanukah/Kwanzaa extravaganza. She left early this morning for New Jersey."

Pacey slapped himself audibly on the forehead. "There goes the betting pool," he muttered to Joey. "And I'm out thirty bucks for the Krispy Kremes."

Conversations broke out all over the auditorium and the mayor had to hold his hands up for quiet, a gesture that was roundly ignored. Finally, Serena Rudman's young voice broke through the cacophony.

"But that isn't fair! This is only our second day to rehearse. How are we supposed to do the show without Muffy?"

The mayor regarded the little girl. "I don't recall asking your opinion, Miss."

"Thank God someone's teaching that kid some manners," Joey whispered to Pacey. "What a brat."

Sundae suddenly stepped forward, and the auditorium quieted as she cleared her throat loudly. "Well then. I think it's patently obvious that responsibility for the Capeside Follies falls to me," she said, ignoring the mayor's comment to her sister. "After all, I am the stage manager and second-in-charge."

Her little sister turned and looked at Sundae as if she had just grown a third eye in the middle of her forehead. "No way, Sandi. You don't even have any talent!"

Joey snorted. The kid was obnoxious, but she told it like it was. And there might be a bright side to all this, she figured. It could provide the perfect opportunity for her to get out of being in the Follies. Maybe they'd have to cancel the show.

"The answer, Potter, is no," Pacey said, nudging her in the ribs, as people started to argue all around them about what to do.

"I didn't even say anything!" she protested.

"No, but you think very loudly. The show must go on, even if you have to direct it."

"Forget it."

"It doesn't matter. You're still in this mess with the rest of us."

"Maybe we could bring in another director from New York, or even Boston," Elmo Beard suggested. "You know. A real professional."

Dawson winced. Elmo and his wife Ellen owned a barbershop downtown. They'd done their song and dance act in every Follies since probably the beginning of time. Every year, their act was awful. Sweet, but awful.

"You know, that's an excellent idea!" Pete McCutter exclaimed. Pete had been a drama major at the University of Massachusetts for one year, then had dropped out to come home and take over the family wholesale oil business. He was president of the Capeside Players. At the age of forty-something, he was still considering moving to either New York or Hollywood to pursue his acting career.

"I'm sorry, but I don't see how we could afford a professional director from New York," the mayor explained sheepishly. "We have a rather limited budget. The Weekend of the Whales didn't exactly fill the town's coffers with rev—"

"Like you could actually get a top director to come to Capeside, anyway," Jack McPhee added under his breath. He was sitting in the back with his sister Andie, who nodded agreement. It wasn't like they were offering a director some big unanticipated opportunity.

"You know, I believe I'm the only one here who is currently in a professional theater-training program," Sundae pointed out huffily. "So it seems only right that—"

"Dear, dear Sandi," Pete interrupted. "I think perhaps you're still a little green to carry the full weight of the Follies."

"It's Sundae, not Sandi, and I'm pretty sure I can handle the full weight, Pete."

"Are you going to make us take off our clothes and roll around in yucky stuff like your friends in New York?" Serena asked loudly.

Sundae shot her sister a killer look. "That's different. That's performance art. You'll understand when you're older."

"Well, I for one don't want my child exposed to someone who does that sort of thing," one of the other stage mothers huffed, pulling her son closer to her. "Capeside Follies always was a family show, and it is going to remain a family show."

"Might I remind everyone that I'm something of a professional," Pete ventured.

"At what?" Sage asked. "Selling overpriced home heating oil to us?"

There was an audible gasp in the auditorium. People had been complaining since the fall about the rising cost of home heating oil, and Pete had taken a lot of the blame.

Pete gathered himself up to his full five feet six. "We're talking about theater, not home heating oil. I'm not a member of OPEC, last time I checked. But I was in one of *The Karate Kid* sequels, if you recall."

"You were an extra," Sage spat.

"I beg to differ. I was an under-five. I had lines. There's a difference."

"Well, Joey Potter had an actual role in that slasher movie they filmed here," Bill Curtson reminded everyone. "I mean, she had scenes with the star and everything. I'd say that makes her the one with the most experience."

All eyes turned to Joey.

Joey was horrified. "Oh, no, not me. I couldn't." She waved her arms in front of her to emphasize her refusal.

"Why not?" Elmo asked. "It's for your town."

"I have a difficult enough time directing my own day. I think taking on the Follies is a little out of my league."

"I second that," Sundae sniffed, as loud discussion broke out again.

Dawson looked at Andie, who had helped direct a school show. She saw him, and drew a finger across her throat, telling him to forget it, she wasn't going to take the gig. Then she made the same motion at Pacey.

Dawson sighed. This was going nowhere fast, and they were no closer to figuring out what to do about the show than they had been twenty minutes before.

Finally, Pacey stood up on a bench. "People? If I might have your attention?"

He waited until they quieted down. "I think there is only one very obvious solution to our dilemma. And his name is . . . Dawson Leery. Allow me to enumerate the reasons."

"Don't you dare," Dawson said to Pacey, but his friend ignored him.

"One: He has proven himself as a professional director by winning various awards for his films, one of which appeared in the Boston Film Festival." Pacey ticked off a finger on one hand. "Two: He's more than familiar with the Winter Follies and would not have to be brought up to speed. And three: I have reason to believe his fee is decidedly within our budget. In other words, we can get him dirt cheap. I know that Dawson will do it for Capeside, because the Leerys have been such an important part of Capeside for so long. Won't you, Dawson?"

Dawson sat tight-lipped, as many people turned to stare at him. He knew he couldn't very well say no.

"You could direct the Follies and film it, too," Serena told him. "You could make me a star!"

Sundae threw her hands up in disgust. "Unbelievable. Dawson is just a high school kid. This is ridiculous."

Joey leaned over to her. "Funny how you didn't think so when you were inviting him for that long weekend in New York," she whispered.

The mayor frowned. Then he made a decision. "Are there any other nominations for the position of director?" he asked. "The fee will be four hundred dollars. I believe that the names of Sandi—"

"Sundae," Sundae corrected.

"Sundae, Dawson Leery, and Pete McCutter are in nomination. Anyone else?"

Silence.

"Then, I believe a show of hands is in order," the mayor pronounced. "All those who favor having Sundae direct the Follies, raise your hand."

Seven hands went into the air.

"All those who favor Pete McCutter?"

Apparently, anger about the cost of heating oil was overwhelming. For there was just one hand waving in the air. Pete's.

"All those who favor Dawson Leery?" Dozens of hands were lifted high.

"Hey, that's not fair. What about none of the above?" Sundae protested. But it was too late.

"Your new director is Dawson Leery," the mayor pronounced. "I know that you will give him the same cooperation that you would give Muffy, and I know that together you are going to make this year's Capeside Follies a show to remember. Dawson? Capeside is grateful to you."

The mayor beckoned to him, and Dawson slowly made his way to the front to take his outstretched hand. A few people applauded. But it was now official. He had shaken the mayor's hand on it.

There was no possible way he could say no.

"Do we really have to have Mr. Gooch's comedy act right after Bethany and Bruce Bowers do the death scene from *Romeo and Juliet?* Andie asked Dawson.

"I agree," Pacey cracked. "That's two comedy routines in a row."

Dawson's head was pounding. It was later that evening. When the meeting in the auditorium had broken up, Dawson had assured the cast and the mayor that, by the next evening's rehearsal, he'd have everything under control and rehearsals would pick up again right where they'd left off.

"When does Christmas vacation begin?" Dawson asked.

"Friday night," Pacey told him. "And the show is ten days after that."

"What day is today?"

"Monday."

"That's what I thought." Dawson buried his head in his hands. "Let's face it, everyone. What we have on our hands is the biggest mess since *Battleship Earth.* And we don't have Travolta."

"Whatever you say, sir," Jen mock saluted him. "You're the director."

Since the end of rehearsal, he and his friends had been up in his bedroom, trying to figure out what to do for the show. Two half pizzas, the pizza boxes filled with leftover bits of crust, lay on Dawson's rug. Pacey was hogging the jumbo bag of Hershey's Kisses, the silver wrappers from the candy had been balled up and shot onto Dawson's bed. Dawson sat cross-legged on the bed next to Joey, while Pacey, Jen, Andie, and Jack lolled on the floor.

As for stage manager Sundae, she was boycotting

the meeting. She'd told Dawson that she would abide by her arrangement with the town and help at rehearsal, but that Dawson couldn't expect her to do anything else without augmenting her salary.

Before he left the auditorium, Dawson had picked up a list of the acts that had already been accepted into the Capeside Follies. Maybe Muffy was being benevolent, or maybe she knew that she'd be leaving, but she had put into this year's show just about everyone who had come forward to say that they had an act to perform.

"Forty-one acts," Joey reminded Dawson. She had just finished counting them again. "Even at three minutes each, we're looking at a show that will run more than two hours."

"But Elmo and Ellen alone are worth ten minutes," Pacey opined. "How do I know this? Because I was studying my watch through their whole act last year. As I recall, my life passed before my eyes multiple times."

"Okay, okay," Dawson said. "I get the picture. Let's just try to figure out the order that will be least painful for our audience. Those seats in the auditorium get awfully hard awfully fast. So far the only suggestions we have are asking three different vocal acts if they'd be willing to perform together."

"One rap, one Christmas carol, and one Broadway medley," Jen said. "Should be interesting. How about we cut the Bowerses? Tragedy doesn't exactly fit the tone."

"Great, Jen. Tell you what, you tell them," Dawson said. "They have their hearts set on *Romeo and*

Juliet. Bruce is already sewing their costumes. And they're the ones who supply my parents' restaurant with beverages and cleaning supplies."

"Okay, scratch that, the duet is in. But we can definitely ax the horrible 'Clementine' number, can't we?" Jack asked. "People will thank us for it into the next millennium."

"Agreed," Jen said.

"Everyone?" Dawson asked.

Heads nodded all around.

He drew a slash through the number on his master list. "One cut down, twelve to go, if we want to bring the Follies in under a butt-numbing two hours."

"You think Muffy did this on purpose?" Pacey wondered. "You know, to get back at us for betting on her new and improved body parts all these years?"

"I have no idea," Dawson replied, "but I do know that we're going to have to find a way to make the cuts and at the same time convince those cut that we're not being cruel and capricious about it."

Andie took a handful of chocolate candies. "Look, let's face it guys. There's no way to cut twelve numbers from the show without a whole lot of people's feelings getting hurt. The only solution is a lottery."

"Like the short story we studied in English?" Joey asked guardedly. "You know how that turned out."

"You know what I mean," Andie continued. "Everyone's act goes into a hat, someone gets blindfolded, and the six who get picked out of the hat are cut."

"I thought we were cutting twelve. Anyway, that'll go over like the proverbial lead balloon," Jack said.

Andie popped a chocolate into her mouth. "You have a better suggestion?"

"I do," Joey said, bringing her knees up to her chin and circling them with her arms. "Maybe, anyway."

"Go ahead, Joey. I'd welcome any suggestion at this point," Dawson said.

Joey nodded. "The whole point of the Follies is town spirit, everyone doing something together at Christmas time, isn't it?"

Nods all around.

"So, it seems to me that everyone in Capeside would find a too-long show preferable to the hurt that would be caused by the slash-and-burn approach. The only solution is that we let the show run for two hours. Which is why we need to add an intermission."

"We've never had an intermission," Dawson pointed out. "Plus the audience might leave in droves at the first opportunity."

"Expand your mind, Dawson," Joey suggested. "It's a new century. New century, new show. This year, we have an intermission. No one is going to leave because they know that their friends, neighbors and family members are all in the big surprise finale."

"Is that the sum total of your brilliant idea?" Andie asked.

"No," Joey said. "There's more. We get people to bake stuff. And during the intermission, we sell baked goods in the lobby."

"For charity?" Jen asked her.

"Of course. For Capeside Special Olympics or some other cause. What do you think?"

The room was silent for a moment. Then Jen shot her a look of admiration. "I have to hand it to you, Joey. That's great."

Joey smiled. "Thanks."

"Or, on second thought, we could donate it to Muffy Smitham," Pacey suggested. "For next year's cosmetic enhancements. On third thought, after what she put us through, let 'er sag."

"I do believe you just saved the butts of everyone in Capeside," Dawson told Joey, grinning, "and made money for charity on top of that. What a girl." He leaned over and hugged her.

Jen eyed Dawson and Joey on the bed. "Highly reminiscent of old times," she remarked.

Joey pulled away from Dawson. "I seem to recall you spent some time up close and personal in this very room yourself, Jen."

"On that very bed," Jen agreed sweetly. "Why, yes. I seem to recall that, too. How about you, Dawson?"

"Hey, it's snowing again!" Andie was standing at the window. She opened it and stuck her head out, to better see the snow coming down.

Unseen, Pacey sneaked up behind her and gave her the tiniest push, but caught her instantly as she screamed, his arms around her waist. She turned around and punched his bicep.

"So not funny, Pacey."

"Ow." Pacey rubbed his arm. "Retaliation is called for. Men, to the battle stations. Snowball fight, guys against girls!"

Laughing and taunting each other, they pulled on their jackets, tumbled down the stairs and outside into the snow. Pacey was already packing a snowball when Jen came up behind him and dumped a fistful of snow down the back of his shirt.

Pacey spun around, a big smile on his face. Without a word, he lifted Jen up and launched her into a nearby snowdrift, where she was buried nearly to the hips. Jen was laughing, and at the same time screaming that Pacey would pay for that.

Before they joined in the battle, Dawson caught Joey's hand. "Thanks," he told her.

"For what?"

"For coming up with the perfect solution. I don't know what I would have done. Maybe you really should be the one directing the Follies, Joey."

She shuddered. "No thanks, Dawson. I leave that in your highly capable hands."

Speaking of hands, she couldn't help noticing. That once more, hers was still in his.

Chapter 4

*H*appiness is two kinds of ice-cream!

Serena Rudman might be a small girl, but she certainly had a loud voice. Dawson sat in the fourth row of the auditorium, listening to her blast out the lyrics to her song. He held up his hands, indicating that she should stop singing and that the pianist should stop playing.

Chester stopped playing, but Serena kept right on going, until she noticed Dawson staring at her. Then, she quit abruptly. "What's wrong?" she asked. "I was right in the middle of my number."

"It's ten past nine," Dawson told her. "Rehearsal ends at nine o'clock. You've sung the song twice and it's in great shape. Take a break, save your voice. We're through until tomorrow."

"Excuse me, Dawson, but the least you could do is to let her finish," Sage Rudman called from the back of the theater. "You broke her concentration."

Dawson craned around and picked Mrs. Rudman out of the crowd. "Mrs. Rudman, I have total faith that your daughter can re-create her powers of concentration at tomorrow's rehearsal."

Without a word, Serena stalked off the stage. Dawson turned to his cast. "Thank you for your cooperation, everyone. And thanks for the idea about the blind auction, Pete. We'll work that in, too."

Pete McCutter gave Dawson a quick wave. "Just trying to help out."

It was the next evening. Dawson had started rehearsal by laying out his plans for a two-act Capeside Follies, with an intermission bake sale taking place in the hallways of the high school between acts. Though some of the old-timers objected on the grounds that the Winter Follies had always been done in one act, most everyone thought it was a really good idea, especially because it guaranteed that their particular routine wouldn't get cut from the show.

Then, out of the blue, Pete had suggested that as long as they were doing a bake sale, why not conduct a blind auction at the same time? He was sure that Capeside's businesses would be happy to donate items for the auction. In fact, he'd be the first one to donate—500 gallons of home heating oil, delivered, to the highest bidder.

Everyone had thought that was a great idea.

Though Dawson immediately suspected that Pete was simply trying to resuscitate his reputation as a businessman, he figured it was for a good cause.

Almost immediately, others shouted out their donations: a dozen hardcover novels from the Book Nook; a half-dozen free haircuts from Elmo Beard; a month of lawn service from Bill Curtson.

"Same time tomorrow, then," Dawson told his cast. "Good job tonight."

As people started to straggle away, Dawson saw his friends gathering by the doors. That afternoon, they made plans to ice skate together at the outdoor rink on the town green after rehearsal.

Dawson rubbed the back of his neck and shook his head wearily. Frankly, he felt too tired even to think about skating.

"Dawson?"

He turned around and saw the mayor of Capeside waiting to talk to him.

"I wanted to congratulate you, Dawson," the mayor said, coming toward him. "You handled that beautifully. I was in the back for the last hour of rehearsal."

"Thank you, sir," Dawson said. "But actually it was Joey Potter's idea to—"

"Yes, yes, I'm sure everyone is contributing," the mayor said, waving off the rest of Dawson's sentence. "I must say, Dawson, that new finale you're working on—'A Capeside Christmas Through History'—well, it brings a tear to this old fool's eyes."

A tear? Dawson smiled inwardly. Frankly, the

finale was so sugarcoated it made his teeth hurt just to rehearse it. But he hadn't yet found a way to tell Elmo, Ellen, and Chester, who had composed it together, that it needed a top-to-bottom rewrite. Not that he was about to tell the mayor that. Instead, he politely thanked the mayor again.

"Incidentally, Dawson, I have some very exciting news that might be interesting to you," the mayor said. "It concerns our show."

"Muffy got sick of New Jersey and decided to come back?" Dawson guessed hopefully.

"Bigger. A lot bigger." The mayor looked this way and that, to make sure no one was listening. He leaned close to Dawson. "Keep this under your hat, all right? I got a call at my office this afternoon from the theater production offices of Arthur and Leonard in New York City. I know Arthur from back in college. We were in the same fraternity at Dartmouth. He was quite the prankster." The mayor's eyes danced as he recalled some college prank or another, and Dawson nodded politely. But he was utterly and completely clueless as to where the mayor might be going with this.

"You may recall that Arthur and Leonard produced the show *Helen!* on Broadway some years back," the mayor continued. "The musical about Helen Keller, with the rock star Nancy Pumpkin in it? Never saw it myself."

Dawson didn't recall it, but the mayor pressed on. "Anyway, Arthur and Leonard have been engaged by a major theater in New York City to create a

Christmas pageant next season. A real family show, with real family values. Right on Broadway itself!"

"Okay," Dawson said, unable to figure out what this had to do with him.

"Not a fancy, Broadway Christmas pageant, but an old-fashioned, small-town Christmas pageant, for all the small-town tourists who come to New York City for the holidays and who might be nostalgic for what they're missing at home."

"With all due respect, sir, if that's what they want, why don't they just stay home in the first place?" Dawson asked.

"Because then they wouldn't be in New York."

Uh-huh. That made no sense at all, but Dawson was not about to argue with the mayor.

"Last year, at Dartmouth homecoming, I mentioned to Arthur that right here in Capeside we put on the most marvelous, touching, totally professional Christmas show. Which is why I think he called me. Are you putting two and two together here, Dawson?"

No. It couldn't possibly be what the mayor seemed to be implying.

"You're kidding," Dawson said, gape-mouthed. "Arthur and Leonard are interested in coming to see the Capeside Follies?"

"And if they like it, to bring it to Broadway," the mayor confirmed gleefully. "Next season."

"But sir," Dawson began, "our pageant is really not ready for Broadway . . . I mean, it's really not the kind of thing that—"

"Don't underestimate our little show, Dawson.

Arthur and Leonard don't. Remember, the show is supposed to be higher on heart than on talent. Which is why they will both be here on opening night."

"But—we only do one performance," Dawson protested. "Opening night is the same thing as closing night!"

"Think of it, Dawson, one grand shot at the big-time for little Capeside. Imagine the possibilities."

Dawson knew that the mayor wanted him to be excited, but actually, he was aghast. No matter how much rehearsal they could pack into the ten days between now and opening night, he knew that the Capeside Winter Follies was about as ready for Broadway as Serena was to solo at Carnegie Hall.

"Sir, I really don't think it's a good idea to—"

"No need to tell me it's a long shot, Dawson," the mayor said, ruefully. "I know that. But it's the Christmas season, remember? Time of miracles. Right?"

"Yes, sir."

"I'll leave it to you to decide when to tell your cast the big news, all right?"

"Uh, fine."

The mayor positively strutted away, beaming at the possibilities, and left Dawson standing alone at the front of the auditorium.

"Dawson, you coming?" Andie called to him. "We're ready to go."

Dawson was a little dazed as he made his way over to his friends. "You are not going to believe what the mayor just told me."

"He's having a sex change operation," Pacey guessed, "and marrying my brother, Doug."

47

"Less likely than that, even."
Dawson told them everything.

The pond was full of lively night skaters clad in bright colors, the ice lit up by small pink and gold lights that surrounded the pond. Tinny music played through an ancient sound system, and orange traffic cones on the ice set up a circular skateway.

Joey and Dawson were skating side-by-side. "I still can't quite grasp it, Dawson," Joey said. "I mean, has the mayor suddenly become delusional?"

"People tend to be blind when it comes to things they love, I suppose," Dawson said.

"Or places," Joey added.

"Or people." His eyes slid over to Joey. She felt his gaze, but very deliberately did not slide her eyes back. Looking directly into Dawson's eyes could be an extremely dangerous thing at times. Everything they both felt always seemed to be written on their faces, and the eyes were the biggest giveaway of all.

"It's beginning to look a lot like Christmas!" As Andie passed by them, she sang along with the sound system at the top of her lungs. "Come on, you guys, join in!"

Pacey was right behind her. "And drown out the sheer poetry of your dulcet tones, McPhee?" he called.

"I can't sing and you know it," Andie said, laughing.

"You have other winning qualities," he assured her, catching up to her, spinning around, and skating backward.

"I used to think they were so perfect together," Dawson mused, as he watched the two of them skate, now side-by-side.

"That was a long time ago, Dawson," Joey reminded him. "A very long time ago."

"Right. Even before there was a you and Pacey."

She wouldn't look in his direction. "I think, Dawson, that is a conversation that neither of us wants or needs to have right now."

"Agreed. Who knows? Maybe Jen and Pacey will live happily ever after. Or, let's see, me and Andie. Or how many other permutations of coupling can we concoct, Joey? It's all so seventies, isn't it? *Bob and Carol and Ted and Alice.*"

Joey deliberately skated away from him, and Dawson instantly regretted what he'd said. What was the point, really, to be bitter? It didn't change anything, or make it all less confusing. And it was Christmastime. Couldn't he just wait until the holidays were over? It wasn't like the rest of Joey's life was so wonderful or so easy.

Dawson's eyes were on Joey's retreating back as he felt an arm link through his. "Care for a skate, sailor?" Jen asked. Her cheeks were flushed red. She looked very cute.

"Sure."

She cocked her head at him as they skated. "That was a very unsure 'sure.' Something happen with Joey?"

"We are an icebound hotbed of teen angst, Jen," Dawson replied. "As such, something is always happening with Joey."

"True. But for once, let's not talk about it."

"Agreed. 'Tis the season for denial, tra-la-la." Jen spun around on her skates and took Dawson's hand, skating backward.

"I'm impressed," Dawson said, laughing. "Where did a city girl like you learn a major frozen pond move like that?"

"It's called the rink at Rockefeller Center, Dawson. Heavy on the tourists, more expensive skating ensembles, like that. One Olympic hopeful always showing off for the cameras of the *Today* show. It would be fun to go there with you sometime."

"I'll take you up on that, Jen."

"Good. And now for my major show-off move, which proves that my parents paid for a year of overpriced lessons when I decided I wanted to be Tara Lipinski absent the bread-and-water diet."

She dropped his hands, skated a few strides, then jumped and twirled in the air, landing in a perfect glide.

Dawson applauded, Pacey waved his arms over his head and whistled through his teeth.

"You go, girl!" Jack called to her. "Five-nine from the American judge, five-two from the Russian. Puts you in third place overall."

"Thank you, thank you, please, no autographs," Jen called back to them.

"Jennifer!"

Jen dug the tips of her figure skates into the ice and came to a quick stop. She watched, astonished, as her grandmother, clad in old-fashioned skates that had to be thirty years old, glided toward her on the ice, a homemade woolen scarf billowing behind her with each stroke of her skate blades.

Ever since Jen had moved to Capeside to escape her wild past in New York, she'd been living next door to Dawson with her extremely religious grandmother. They hadn't been close before Jen had come to Capeside, and it had taken a long time in Capeside before Jen could warm up to her mother's mother, who sometimes seemed to be from a different planet than she was. Sometimes, Grams drove Jen crazy. But other times, Jen thought Grams was probably one of the most remarkable people on the planet.

Sometimes, she thought both things at once.

"Grams, what a nice surprise!" Jen hugged her grandmother warmly. "I was showing off."

"Yes, I saw, dear. Nice single Salchow. Very well executed."

"Thanks, Grams." They began smoothly skating side-by-side clockwise, mixing right in with the other skaters. "Did you come out here to see me in action, to see how Mom's lessons for me worked out?"

"Not exactly, Jennifer."

"Just a sudden yen to hit the ice, then? Thinking about trying out for the Olympic hockey team?"

"Not that, either." Grams skated silently for a few moments. "To tell you the truth, Jennifer, I just had rather a distressing phone call."

Jen stopped skating. "What's the matter? Is someone sick?"

"No—"

"Worse? Was it from my parents?"

51

"Yes, your parents called. Well, your mother, to be more specific."

Jen grabbed Grams's arm, a sick feeling welling up in her stomach. "Was there an accident? What's wrong with her?"

"I'm afraid only a battalion of psychotherapists could answer that one for us, dear. I didn't mean to alarm you. She's perfectly fine. The thing is—"

"Would you please just tell me, Grams? You're making me very nervous."

"Yes, I suppose I am."

"Just tell me."

"Well, here it is, then. Your mother called, Jennifer. She wants you to come home for Christmas. In fact, she expects me to put you on a train a week from Monday. She's meeting you at Grand Central Station."

Chapter 5

Dawson sat in the middle of the theater and slumped down in his seat, as Nan Lynn Hornsby, the show's choreographer, went through the dance routine with the entire cast for the big finale, "A Capeside Christmas Through History."

Nan and her husband had moved out of Capeside six years earlier and retired to Hilton Head, South Carolina. But everyone still talked about the years that Nan had choreographed the group musical numbers as the very best years of the Follies.

It had been Gale's idea for Dawson to call Nan and basically beg her to come back home for the first Follies of the new century, now that he was going to direct the show. Had Muffy been in Capeside, she would have handled both the directing and the choreography, but Dawson had never made up a dance step in his life.

To Dawson's shock and relief, Nan had agreed to return to Capeside and choreograph the show. She booked the last room at the Capeside Inn.

Estimates put Nan at roughly the same age as Muffy. Her claim to fame had been her brief employment as a Rockette at Radio City Music Hall in New York, and as she was fond of saying, "I still have the gams to prove it." She proved this by wearing miniskirts, and added drama to her outfits with her garish beads and jewelry.

"And right and left and cha-cha step, cha-cha step, turn and turn and kick and kick!" Standing in front of the cast, Nan called out the moves and demonstrated them at the same time. Behind her, four dozen people of all ages were gamely attempting to keep up with her.

This was Nan's second rehearsal with the cast. She'd taught them the steps for the finale yesterday, but apparently pretty much everyone had forgotten them overnight. Jen and Pacey kept cracking each other up and messing each other up on purpose. Joey was off to the side, keeping up better than most. Jack had dropped out completely.

But Andie seemed to know almost all the steps and executed them with style and flair. Dawson was both surprised and impressed. He couldn't recall Andie ever mentioning that she had had dance training. Next to Andie, eight-year-old Serena had managed to wedge herself in front and center, and she, too, knew almost all the steps. In fact, Dawson could see some of the adults watching the little girl and copying her moves.

"And here's where you sing again, but for now we'll just work on the steps," Nan explained, still marching to the beat. "We form three lines and march in place and march and march and march."

Dawson sank down even farther in his chair. Chester and his compatriots had written a variation on the Woody Guthrie song "This Land Is Your Land," except with specific lyrics about Capeside. This was going to be the new finale, replacing "Clementine."

For the life of him, Dawson could not imagine half of his cast remembering both the dance steps and the lyrics. Arthur and Leonard have no idea what they're in for, Dawson thought. If they want a show big on heart instead of talent, they're coming to the right place.

Thus far, Dawson had only told his friends about the Broadway producers coming to Capeside to scout the Follies. They'd all found the notion both ludicrous and hilarious. But Dawson couldn't help but notice that ever since, they'd also seemed much more intense during rehearsals. Almost as if they took seriously the idea that anyone would have any interest in moving the Follies to Broadway.

But that couldn't be. Could it?

Sundae slid her skinny self into the seat next to Dawson. "Break in five minutes."

"Good. It will put me out of the misery of watching those poor people attempt to do Nan's choreography."

"Who knew we lived in a town of people with a total lack of rhythm?"

"Me," Dawson replied. "However, it never bothered me before, because I was not responsible for it."

Sundae patted his hand. "Cheer up, Dawson. No one will expect anything other than the most pathetic Christmas show this year, since it's being directed by a kid in high school. The town's expectations are even lower than usual."

"I assume you intended that to sting, Sundae, but frankly, right now, I would gladly turn this production over to you."

Sundae eyed him coldly. "Is that so? Good. Do it. I'll have this show one hundred percent improved in under forty-eight hours."

"Tempting, but impossible. I'm in charge and I'm responsible. And I don't quit."

"Fine, have it your way," Sundae snapped. "Just to keep you in the loop, then, Mr. Director, I gave the cast a few notes earlier. I told Elmo and Ellen Beard that since the town has suffered through their exact same excruciating song and dance act for who knows how many years, if they can't come up with something new, we're cutting them from the show."

"You *what?*"

"I also gave Bethany and Bruce a few notes on their scene from *Romeo and Juliet*. Let's face it, he comes across so drag queen that it makes the scene comic."

"But that's—"

"I asked him to work on deepening his voice placement and also suggested he keep his hips still when he crosses, so much more butch. He got all huffy, but—whatever. Oh, and I told Serena to can the precious little hand gestures she uses when she sings—way too Baby Jane, if you know what I mean, and—"

Dawson was furious, but he worked to keep his voice steady. "Time out, Sundae. Query: who authorized you to give the cast notes?"

"Answer: the stage manager often gives notes, Dawson. That's how it's done in professional theater. In New York. Where I go to school."

"Agreed. But in professional theater, said notes come from the director, unless they're technical."

Sundae rolled her eyes. "Well, if you're going to nit-pick."

"Do not ever, and I mean *ever*, do that again." Dawson was supremely irritated.

"Oh, let's not take our little high school self too seriously, Dawson. You know, come to think of it, I'm willing to co-direct this piece with you. Together, I really believe that I could—"

"Dawson, we're going to take it from the top again," Nan called from the stage. "I think it's coming along, finally."

"Great, go to it." Dawson hoped he sounded more enthusiastic than he felt.

Nan turned to the cast. "All right, Chester, everyone, let's take it from the top—"

Sundae stood up and called, "Sorry, Nan. Break time. Take ten, everyone."

As people ran for water or sank down in the nearest spot, Nan strode down the aisle to confront

Sundae, a long pink chiffon scarf trailing behind her.

"I am perfectly capable of calling my own breaks when I am ready to call my breaks," she fumed at the stage manager.

"They were due for one. I'm stage manager. It's my job to call breaks."

"Oh, really? May I see your union card?"

Sundae looked confused. "My what?"

"Union card. Actors Equity Association. If you're not in the union, then you do not call union breaks. I was a card-carrying member of Actors Equity, SAG, AFTRA, Society of Stage Directors and Chore-ographers—"

"That was in another century, Nan," Sundae reminded her. "Literally. Your time—brief as it was—has come and is now long, long gone. Sad to say, even your legs are finally starting to go."

"Dawson, I have never been so insulted in my life. Do something about this witch!" Nan was furious.

"All right. I will." Dawson turned to Sundae. "You're fired."

"*What?*"

"What part of 'you're fired' is it that you don't understand, exactly?"

"You can't fire me," Sundae sputtered. "Who the hell do you think you are?"

"The director of Capeside Winter Follies. And as of this moment, you are the former stage manager of Capeside Winter Follies."

"And just who do you think is going to call the tech cues on your show if you fire me?"

"You will find that in show business, no one is irreplaceable," Nan put in.

Sundae grabbed her purse. "Fine. Good. I am so out of here. Your show is going to suck, Dawson, because you are in way, way over your head. When you wreck Winter Follies, and everyone in town is either crying or laughing at you, I'll be the one you hear laughing the loudest."

"Have a nice day, dear," Nan called, as Sundae strode furiously down the aisle.

"Reasonably good exit speech," Dawson noted. "A bit over the top on the histrionics, but, all things considered, decently done."

"Don't let her undermine your confidence, Dawson," Nan said kindly. She did a high kick with her right leg. "And my legs are not going. You can't do this if your legs are going."

An hour later, Dawson sat with Jen in the prop room backstage. The green room was full of people, as was the auditorium itself, and he wanted to talk to Jen alone.

He'd just asked her to drop out of the show so that she could be his stage manager.

"I can't say I'm sorry you fired Sundae's anorexic ass," Jen admitted, unwrapping her tuna sandwich, "but stage managing? I have to admit, Dawson, much to my own surprise I've been getting into performing in the show."

"I wouldn't ask you," Dawson told her, "if I had a decent alternative."

"Jack? Andie? Pacey? Joey?" she ticked off. "Any

of the old-timers? Any one of them is more than capable of taking on the task."

"Frankly, I tried to get Jack, but he turned me down flat. He's too busy. He's now in charge of building the set."

"Who was in charge before?"

"No one," Dawson admitted. "So I jumped at his offer to do it. Andie's performing. She has her heart set on doing that ventriloquism thing. It hasn't been done before; it should be funny. Pacey Witter is not exactly the name that springs to mind when I think of someone I can one hundred percent count on to run the show backstage, which leaves—"

"Either me or Joey." She took another bite of her sandwich. "Just out of curiosity, Dawson, did you ask everyone before getting to me?"

"I'm asking you first. I was just sharing my mental processing."

"How very Dawson of you. And my last question is, why not Joey?"

Dawson had no idea, except that the idea made him wildly uncomfortable. And he didn't know why. "It didn't seem a wise choice," he said carefully.

"Enigmatic. Also very Dawson of you. What's up with you two, anyway?"

"You mean today, as opposed to yesterday? This week, as opposed to last week? Which episode of our ongoing soap opera are we on?"

"Will Dawson and Joey end up in each other's arms?" Jen asked, mock-dramatically. "Will Pacey come between them again? Will Jen? Like sands through the hourglass pass the—"

"If I was not a major player in that scenario, I'd find it very amusing, but as it is . . ."

There was no need for him to finish the sentence. What he meant was painfully obvious.

Jen swallowed the last bite of her sandwich. "You know what's funny, Dawson? That I'm here at all, and that we're having this conversation. Because my mom called. She wants me to, as she put it, 'come home for Christmas.' "

Dawson gulped. Not only would that eliminate Jen as stage manager, but he knew that Jen and her mother had a very scratchy relationship. "What did you tell her?"

"I called her back and told her I already was home for Christmas."

"Although it is hardly in my self-interest to say this, don't you want to spend the holiday with your mother? That is, if she's making the overture to you, I mean?"

"What do you think, Dawson? That she listened to me? That she cares about my feelings?" Jen crumpled her plastic wrap into a ball and threw it at the trashcan. It missed, and fell to the floor. "We had a huge fight on the phone. She insisted. And her rebellious daughter refused to bow to her wishes."

"I see," Dawson said, not knowing what else to say.

"Good answer, Dawson. One deserves another. The answer to your question is yes, Dawson. It wasn't any fun singing in the Follies without you, anyway. And it still wouldn't be any fun to spend

Christmas with my mother. Not this year. So congrats. You just got yourself a new stage manager."

Onstage, Nan was going over the soft-shoe break with Elmo and Ellen. She'd gently offered to choreograph it for them and they'd jumped at the opportunity. Chester was pounding out "You Can't Take That Away From Me" on the piano as they danced. Meanwhile, in the back of the theater, Andie was rehearsing with her ventriloquist's dummy when Pacey strolled over.

"You're a woman of mystery, McPhee," Pacey said, keeping his voice low. "What prompted you to take up this particular talent?"

"I was eight and saw it on *Sesame Street*. I took lessons for two years at the YMCA."

"And here I thought I knew everything about you."

"Not even close, Pacey," the dummy squawked. "Forget it, dude."

Pacey laughed hard. He eyed the freckle-faced boy dummy. "What's the dummy's name?"

"Witty," Andie said. "I thought about making it Witter, but I like a dash of subtlety with my art."

"Well, you're as subtle as a Mack truck," Witty squawked at Andie.

"Did I say you could say anything?" Andie said to him.

"I wasn't aware I needed permission," the dummy replied haughtily.

Pacey laughed. "I gotta tell you, McPhee, that's kind of freaky."

"Freak!" Witty's eyes bulged out of his head by some invisible control Andie pushed, and his head spun around like Linda Blair in *The Exorcist*. "You had your shot at her, buddy, now she's my woman, so back off!" Pacey cracked up, as Bill Curtson approached the two of them.

"You know, that dummy looks just like you, Witter," Bill noted, also keeping his voice low, though Chester was famous for pounding on the piano so loudly that it was difficult to hear over his playing. "Except for the freckles and the bulging eyes, I mean."

"You think, Bill?" was all that Pacey replied. He didn't want to get into an argument with the guy.

Andie pushed something in the back of the dummy and Witty's eyes settled back into their sockets.

"You sure have a lot of talent, Andie," Bill said admiringly. "I was watching."

"Thanks."

Bill shoved his hands deep into his pockets. "I mean, on top of everything else, you're like the best dancer in the show."

Andie grinned. "Thanks, Bill." She didn't mind at all that Bill was flirting with her in front of Pacey. In fact, she was rather enjoying it.

"Hey, you wanna grab some coffee or something after rehearsal?"

"That'll be pretty late. Andie's not much of a night person," Pacey said, intervening. "I'm warning you, she'll fall asleep into her double latte. Even a chocolate bomb brownie won't keep her awake."

"Hey, dude, she's perfectly capable of speaking for

herself," Witty squawked at Pacey. Pacey blanched, and then blanched more when the dummy actually winked at him.

Andie turned to Bill. "I'd love to go for coffee with you. And a brownie."

Bill's face lit up. "Yeah? Really? Great! So, um, catch you later." He hurried off, and even from behind he looked happy.

"Nice of the two of you to make his night," Pacey said, watching Bill depart. "What is that, a mercy coffee date?"

Andie set Witty carefully down in his velvet-lined box, and closed it. "What makes you think I don't genuinely like him?"

"Wild guess. You've got your application to Harvard completed a year early, and he has the functional IQ of a desiccated pea pod." Pacey's eyes were still on Bill. He didn't turn to Andie until Bill was out the doors of the auditorium.

"Well, in that case, I'll have to learn to appreciate his other qualities," Andie said lightly. "Quite the buns on him, huh?"

Pacey's jaw fell open. "What did you just say?"

"Oh, come on, Pacey," Andie said, gathering her things together. "You and I haven't been together in a long time. You're over me. You want to be friends with me, we're friends. I suggest you get over the past. 'Tis the season to be jolly, not jealous."

"I realize that Witty isn't even on your arm right now, McPhee, and it's really you speaking. But why is it you sound like you're channeling some mindless football jock with crud for brains?"

"Pacey, I—"

Before Andie could answer, someone on the stage screamed. Pacey and Andie whirled around just in time to see Nan lose her balance at the lip of the stage and fall ten feet into the orchestra pit.

Chapter 6

"East Cape Flyers' goal scored by number forty-one, Bill Curtson, assisted by number twenty-four, Chad Berman. Time of the goal, five minutes and twenty-six seconds of the second period!"

"Yes!" Andie cheered from the bleachers, pumping the air with her fist. Jack, who was sitting next to her, gave her an arch look.

"Since when are you such a hockey fan?"

"It's an exciting game—"

"One that you did not know the rules for until a couple of days ago, and which you had never seen a game of until after you went out with Bill a couple of times? How high school."

Andie nudged Jack playfully in the ribs, but kept her eyes on Bill, who was still out on the ice. It was true that she and Bill had gone out twice. And it was also true that she'd formerly shown zero interest in hockey. But she definitely had an interest in Bill.

He was fascinating, really. Pacey had been completely wrong about Bill. He wasn't stupid. It's just that school held very little interest for him. Instead, he was a serious hockey player—one of the guys who awoke every day at four-thirty in the morning to get ice time at the local rink. And he was definitely a really nice guy who was totally into her.

The night before, at Follies rehearsal, he'd invited her to come to watch him play in a district league game at an arena a few miles from Capeside. Bring Jack, he'd suggested. It wasn't any fun to watch a hockey game by yourself. Which was how Andie came to be sitting with Jack at the Falmouth Arena, watching Bill's East Cape Flyers play against a team from Worcester.

"Did you know that Bill is one of the best hockey players his age in the whole state?" Andie asked Jack, as she watched Bill go from offense to defense, skating rapidly down the ice with his teammates.

"Yes, Andie, I do. Because you've told me that twice already since the game started." Bill skated off the ice and another guy took his place.

"Well, that's why we don't see him much at school. He's always practicing, and a lot of times his district team is traveling."

Jack nodded. "And you're into him for his fearless hockey studliness?"

"I'm into him because he's a nice guy. And because of his studliness," she admitted.

Boom! The boards in front of where they were sitting shook, as one of the Flyers' players took a crushing hip check from one of the Worcester defensemen. The Flyer sprawled on the ice and his stick went flying.

"Such a low-key, Zen-like game," Jack joked. "Did Bill mention if the teeth in his mouth sit in a water glass at night? Hockey players are notorious for false teeth, you know. Next time you're in the clinch, see if you can dislodge 'em with your tongue. Just for fun."

"That's disgusting, Jack. Plus, not that it's any of your business, we have not had a 'clinch' yet."

Jack's eyebrows went up. "A buff guy like that?"

Andie grinned at him. "Oh, so you noticed."

"Only in the most objective way."

Jack turned his attention back to the ice, where Bill was skating out for another shift. So did Andie. She had no problem with the fact that her brother was gay. But it still seemed weird to joke about guys with him.

Andie stood up. "Go Flyers!" she shouted, and the Flyers bore in on the Worcester defense. Bill played center on the Flyers' first offensive line, and he seemed to have an uncanny ability to find the open man and then skate into position for a quick wrist shot or a deflection. Now, he deftly stick-handled past one of the defensemen, skated in with the puck behind the goal, and snapped a sharp pass to one of his teammates, who was standing at the blue line.

Bam! The powerful slap shot rocketed toward the

Worcester goaltender, who stuck out his blocker arm, and the puck deflected into the crowd.

"Nice pass, Curtson!" Andie shouted, as Bill and his linesmen skated off the ice, to be replaced by another shift.

" 'Nice pass'?" Jack echoed, bemused. "Maybe you should give the game a try yourself."

"Please," Andie groaned. "This is probably one of my last free social moments until after the Follies."

Every time Andie thought about how Dawson had asked her to take over as choreographer after Nan fell off the stage and sprained her ankle, she got the strangest feeling in her stomach. Both excited and sick. She was thrilled that he'd asked her. But she felt sick most of the time that she was going to screw everything up, even with Nan watching and guiding her.

"So, how's it going, anyway? You haven't told me."

"Sometimes I think it's great," Andie replied. "Other times I wake up in the middle of the night in a cold sweat, certain that I'm ruining everything."

"Andie, you are smart, talented, and a perfectionist. I don't think 'ruining everything' is a very strong possibility."

"I'm also a control freak who overplans," she pointed out. "And on top of that, I know my shortcomings."

Down on the ice, play had stopped, and two of the guys on the opposing teams were jawing at each other. The linesmen quickly stepped in between them.

"You okay here?" Jack asked. "Hockey's not really my thing. You got a ride home?"

"Sure and sure. Bill said he'd drop me after the game. The hayride is tonight at eight, right? I was thinking of asking him to come with us."

"Only if he takes a shower," Jack advised his sister.

The annual Capeside hayride always took place at eight o'clock the Friday night that Capeside's public schools let out for Christmas break. It was a big deal. Teams of horses and horse-drawn sleighs assembled on the town green and then took groups of fifteen or twenty people out for a ride around Capeside, stopping in front of the homes that had the most spectacular—and sometimes garish—displays of Christmas lights.

A local department store offered a prize of more Christmas lights to the home that got voted biggest and best display, and sometimes the competition was fierce. The store even gave scorecards to people on the sleighs so that they could cast advisory votes.

"I'll meet you there," Andie said distractedly, because Bill's line was back out on the ice. She stood and waved her fist in the air as Bill took control of the puck and led the rush. She put the Follies firmly out of her mind and jumped to her feet. "Go Flyers, go!"

"Wouldn't you say they overdid it somewhat?" Pacey commented, as the horse-drawn sleigh that carried him, Dawson, and all their friends came to a stop in front of a split-level colonial home on

Widowmaker's Way. The Christmas light display on this house lit up the entire street.

It was nine-thirty that night. Right on schedule, the annual sleigh-ride procession had left the town green at eight, and for the last hour and a half, they'd been gallivanting all over Capeside looking at the Christmas displays. A dusting of snow around six had provided fresh powder for the horses to clomp through, even though the night was now clear, cold, and glorious. There was no moon, so the Milky Way cut a foamy swath through the dark skies above them.

"I'd say that if you don't pull that blanket closer around us," Jen shivered, "that you're going to be delivering me to the emergency room at Falmouth Hospital with a bad case of frostbite. It wasn't this cold last year, as I recall."

Pacey wrapped Jen more carefully in the blanket. "You weren't here for the winter of seventy-seven. Now, *that* was a winter. It got so cold that when my brother Doug tried to lick a lamppost on a dare, they had to call out the National Guard to remove his tongue."

"You weren't here, either," Jen reminded him. "Neither was your brother."

"Don't bring up petty details."

"How much longer?" Jen asked.

"I think this is the second to last house. We always finish at the Beards'. They spend as much time on their display as they do practicing for the Follies. Anyway, your lips and nails aren't blue, that's a good sign. Here, drink this."

He unscrewed the cap off a thermos full of hot chocolate and poured her a steaming cup. She smiled gratefully. "Thanks. You just bought me another fifteen minutes."

"So, what do you give this display?" Pacey asked. "On the garish scale, that is."

"Somewhat less than what Jennifer Lopez wore to the Oscars last year, somewhat more than the store windows at Macy's," Jen commented.

"I heard that comment. In my humble opinion, on Christmas, I don't think you can go too over the top," Andie called out. She and Bill were snuggled together under a big wool blanket on the other side of the sled. "That's the fun of Christmas."

Pacey took another dubious glance at the decorated house. It was entirely bedecked in red, white, and blue Christmas lights; they covered it from roof to ground. The fir trees in front were circled by more lights, swirling up to huge silver stars at the top. There was a life-size Santa and eight reindeer near the front door, suspended from guy wires in midair. And to top it all off, a floodlit, gigantic nativity scene with ten-foot-high Wise Men stood not far from the sleigh itself.

"Sheesh," Pacey grimaced. "The electric bill for this must be scary. I'm giving it a two." He took a pencil from his pocket and marked his scorecard.

Dawson and Joey were in the front of the sleigh, just behind the horsemen. While the others were checking out the house, they were flat on their backs, gazing up at the night sky.

"How are you on your constellations, Dawson?"

Joey asked softly. "Because I'd much rather look at the sky than at tacky Christmas lights."

"Tacky Christmas lights, like the Follies, are another cherished Capeside tradition," Dawson reminded her, smiling at the thought. "In fact, don't you remember when we were kids, and the Leerys and the Potters would make an outdoor barbecue together on Christmas Eve, and then our parents used to . . ."

Dawson's voice trailed off as he realized he was about to say something that could really hurt Joey emotionally.

It was true, though. The Leerys and the Potters used to make an outdoor barbecue together on Christmas Eve. There'd be hamburgers and hot dogs and all the things that they'd eat at a barbecue in the summer, except they'd all be bundled up against the cold. They'd have sack races and play horseshoes, even if they had to drive the stakes into the snow. The parents would be drinking eggnog, and Joey and Dawson would have hot cider.

Then, when the meal was done and before they went to church together, they'd put up their own homemade nativity scene on the Leerys' side of the creek and make an enormous snowman on the Potters,' if there was enough snow.

All of this was done on Christmas Eve, and somehow waiting for the Eve itself made everything feel more special.

But that was before.

Before Joey's dad went to prison. Before Joey's mom died. Before a whole bunch of things that only added up to pain for her.

Dawson felt awful. How could he have been so insensitive? "I'm sorry, Joey," he softly. "I'm a complete and total jerk."

Dawson felt the lightest touch of Joey's hand. "It's all right, Dawson. Once something happens, it happens. And you can't stop yourself from remembering, no matter how hard you try, because when you try to stop yourself, it's the same thing as if you'd thought of it. I remember, too."

She pointed up at the sky. "You know that one? The red one?"

Dawson followed Joey's gloved index finger. "Sure. Orion the hunter. It has the belt."

"I remember when you thought you could throw a snowball and hit his belt."

"How could I have been so crazy?" Dawson wondered aloud.

"You weren't crazy," Joey said. She touched his arm again as the sleigh began to move away, toward a house down the street that had an even louder and more flamboyant display of Christmas lights than the one they'd just seen.

"I wasn't?"

"Nope," Joey told him. "Because I completely believed you. Sometimes," she added softly, not looking at him, "I still do."

Chapter 7

"But how can that be?" Joey asked her sister. "The Follies show isn't for another ten days. What are they going to do when they're here visiting?"

"Antiquing. Their wives want to go antiquing," Bessie replied.

"Antiquing? All the antique shops are closed for December!"

Bessie sighed, then lifted a cup of steaming coffee to her lips. "I'm not complaining. It isn't like Potter's B and B is being overwhelmed with Christmas guests. There's plenty of room at the Inn. Especially if we get snow. They say there might be more tomorrow."

It was the morning after the sleigh ride. Joey had slept late on a Saturday morning for the first time in weeks—in fact, it was nearly ten o'clock. She had just come down to eat breakfast with her older sister and her little nephew Alexander. Not only had she slept late that morning, Joey was looking forward to sleeping late for the next several days. After months of both going to school and helping her sister with Potter's B and B, she had plenty of sleep to catch up on, she figured.

All she had to do between now and Christmas was help Dawson with the Follies and work as many shifts at the restaurant as Gale and Mitch would let her.

But it was just not to be. Not this Christmas vacation. Because her sister had just announced to her that Arthur and Leonard, the theater producers from New York, were arriving at the B and B that very afternoon.

"I honestly don't know what they're planning to do here for nine days," Bessie went on, shrugging. "They said they thought it would be fun to spend the week before Christmas here on Cape Cod. Oh, yes. They said they also wanted to go on a day trip to Gloucester."

"The Perfect Storm," Joey muttered. Ever since the movie had come out, they got at least one call a week at the B and B from tourists who wanted to know how close they were to the town where that movie was set. "Not very," Joey always replied.

"Anyway, they've got two rooms beginning tonight. And they're arriving just after lunch."

"So it's a done deal."

Bessie put down her coffee. "Joey, of course I said yes. They're paying a hundred dollars a night each, for nine days, that's eighteen hundred dollars. For that kind of money, I'd take them, their wives, and their pet monkeys if they wanted to bring them. You don't have to work at the restaurant, now."

Joey gave her a look. "They don't have monkeys, do they?"

Bessie smiled. "No. Joey, I know you were looking forward to a break, and I know that you've got rehearsals for the Follies."

"Don't remind me of the Follies," Joey told her. "Now that Arthur and Leonard are staying here, I'll be reminded of it every single minute."

"Look at it this way—they just paid for the repairs we're making on the septic system."

"Wait a sec. Don't these guys have children?" Joey asked sharply. "Don't they have to be home to prepare for Christmas?"

"They're Jewish, they told me," Bessie said. "They even asked me if we had a place where they could put a menorah, since Chanukah starts tonight. I said no candles in the rooms, but if they want to bring an electric one, it's fine with us, and I'd put it in the front window next to the Christmas tree when we put it up."

"When are they checking out?" Joey reached for a piece of buttered toast on a plate in the center of the table and took a bite.

"Right after the Follies show, they're driving back to New York, something about having another show to see the night after," Bessie told her sister. "Now, when you finish breakfast, could you go make up Rooms 2 and 3? And do a good job? Like

I said, they're supposed to arrive right after noon-
time."

Two hours later, Joey was upstairs in Room 2, vac-
uuming, changing the sheets, using vinegar on the
mirror above the dresser, fluffing the pillows, and
making sure that the heat was working. She even
sprayed an aromatherapy spritz for a few moments
so that the room would have the faint scent of san-
dalwood.

She had just finished dusting the antique chair
by the desk when she heard a familiar *beep-beep* in
the driveway. Pacey's truck? What was he doing
here?

She went downstairs and outside. Indeed, Pacey
was behind the wheel of his truck, leading a slow-
motion motorcade into the parking area of the B and
B. Right behind him were two nearly identical SUVs.
One was white, one was black, and attached to the
roofs of each was a full complement of luggage and
sporting equipment—skis, snowshoes, skates, and
the like. There was enough gear atop the SUVs to
support the winter Olympics team of a small Euro-
pean nation.

"Ahoy, Potter!" Pacey called from the front seat of
his truck, as he came to a stop on the gravel.

"Right back atcha," Joey replied, still puzzled as to
why Pacey would be leading a motorcade, but grateful that the snow of earlier in the week had melted,
so there wasn't ice in the driveway for the cars to
contend with.

"You planning on moving in with us?" she asked
him. "What's with the motorcade?"

Pacey grinned and motioned behind him. "In yonder matching Ford Broncos are the celebrated producing team of Arthur and Leonard, direct from the Upper West Side of New York City. Making a very special nine-day appearance in lovely Capeside U.S.A., more or less."

"Don't tell me. You've been hired as their escort for the week?"

"You know, Potter, that's not a bad idea. I'll run it by the boys and see what they think. But for the moment, not hardly. What happened was, they got lost in town, Deputy Doug saw them driving around in circles and went to their assistance. He was too busy solving mass-murder cases, so he called me to get them here."

Joey was tempted to ask how anyone could get lost in Capeside—it wasn't like their town was Manhattan. Instead, she watched quietly as Arthur and Leonard got out of their cars—one from the white Bronco, one from the black one. She had no idea which was which, but the producers made that instantly clear to her.

"Yo Leonard, we're here!" the one who had to be Arthur called to the one who had to be Leonard. "Beautiful Capeside U.S.A., Vacationland of the Universe. Fresh air, ocean breezes, and all that."

"Finally, buddy," Leonard called back. "What a shlep! Where's the closest subway station? I'm ready to go back." He laughed at his own bad joke.

"Anything I can do for you?" Pacey asked them, sticking his head farther out the window of his truck. "I can help you unpack if you need it."

"We got it covered, we need the exercise. Thanks, Pacey. I gotta tell you, no one would have been this courteous to us back in the big bad city," Arthur told him. "Want to be our hired guide to the wild night life of Capeside for a week? Just kidding!"

"Well, that's just how we country bumpkins are," Pacey said, his voice hospitable. "And really, anything I can do to make your stay more pleasant, don't hesitate to call on me or your lovely innkeeper, Miss Potter. I'm out of here."

Pacey gave the producers an exaggerated wave, and Joey couldn't help but grin—not just at how nice Pacey was being to the B and B's new guests, but at Arthur and Leonard themselves.

They were standing together now, side-by-side. And they looked like nothing as much as a semi-colon. Arthur was small—no more than five feet, four inches, Joey guessed. Then she noticed that he had cowboy boots on, which meant he had to be, actually, about five-two. He was slim, with a short, dark beard. As for his partner, Leonard, he towered over Arthur by a good foot. Where Arthur was skinny, Leonard was rotund and out of shape, the open down vest he wore over his jeans and turtleneck sweater only accentuating the roundness of his belly.

"Let's go unload," Arthur told his partner. "Leave the sporting equipment on the SUVs. No one's gonna steal it here."

As they reached their vehicles, their wives got out of the front seats. Joey's eyes widened. Both of them were breathtakingly, movie-star beautiful. Arthur's wife was taller than he was, with the long, lean lines of a dancer and curly red hair to the middle of her back. Leonard's wife was petite and curvy, with a short Winona Ryder–style brunette hairdo. While the producers looked to be Gale and Mitch's age, the two wives both appeared to be about thirty years old.

Arthur took a couple of bags out of the back of the SUV and brought them toward Joey. "Hi!" he said brightly. "I'm Billy Arthur, that other guy over there is my partner Charlie Leonard. But call us Arthur and Leonard. God knows, everyone else does."

Their wives came over to join them, and Joey stood there, waiting for the two producers to introduce the two women to her.

They didn't.

"I'm Joey Potter," she said awkwardly. "My sister Bessie and I will be your innkeepers."

"Great," Leonard said. "Arthur, let's go get the rest of our gear. Girls, go inside and get some hot chocolate."

"Uh, I'll get that for you," Joey managed.

Without another word, the two producers returned to their SUVs to unload their luggage. Meanwhile, Joey led the two producers' wives inside the inn, thinking how odd it was that no one had bothered to even tell her their names.

Capeside is your town
Capeside is my town

From White's Hardware Store
To our real great downtown
From the Town Marina
To the Magic Cleaners
Capeside is made for you and me!

"Sing it out!" Dawson exhorted his cast, that, the next day at rehearsal, was assembled *Rent*-style across the stage in one solid line. "Go right into the final chorus. Give me everything you've got!"

No matter how excruciating I find it, he added mentally, since the lyrics were, in his opinion, perhaps the worse parody lyrics ever written.

Andie had put the cast through their dance steps during the first part of the finale. Then, for the final choruses, she had arranged them so that the kids in the cast were standing in between the adults; the effect, she'd hoped, was to show visually that the young people of Capeside were the town's future.

Dawson didn't know if that was too subtle, but it looked good, anyway. The piano music swelled and modulated up a half-tone, reminiscent of a Barry Manilow arrangement.

We're home to Capeside,
Capeside for Christmas
If we didn't come home,
Capeside would miss us,
Capeside for the sleigh rides,
Capeside for the Fol-lies,

Capeside is made for you and me.
Capeside is made for you and me!

As the song ended, everyone onstage raised their hands above their heads and shouted, "Merry Christmas, Merry Christmas!" as per Dawson's instructions. Dawson attempted a smile, trying to give his cast as much energy as possible.

In addition to the truly horrible lyrics, something wasn't working in the finale. He had a pretty good idea what the problem was. What he didn't know was what to do about it.

He looked at Jen. She was frowning, too. He pointed to his watch. By now, Jen knew what that gesture meant.

"Okay, fifteen-minute break, everyone," she told the cast. "Great job, we'll take it from the top of the second act when we return. Serena, warm up, okay?"

The little girl nodded gratefully as the rest of the cast, glad for a break, scattered. Within a few minutes, the auditorium was empty, except for Dawson, Jen, and Andie.

"Let's hit the green room," he told them all. "I want to talk, and I frankly don't want anyone in the cast to hear."

His friends followed him as he led the way backstage to the motley assortment of couches and chairs that were assembled in the bare storage room that passed for the green room.

"So?" he asked Jen, as soon as he'd plopped down

in one of the seats. "You agree with me that there's a problem?"

Jen nodded. "Big one."

"Agree what?" Andie asked.

"The finale isn't working," Dawson said. "I mean, it's okay, but it isn't really working."

"I think it's fine," Andie countered. "Okay, I admit it's a little hokey, but it's perfect for a perfectly hokey little show, which is exactly what the Follies are."

Dawson shook his head. "No, Andie, there is an acceptable level of hokeyness for the Follies, and the takeoff on "This Land Is Your Land" goes over the line. In fact, way over. I know Chester and his friends put a lot of work into it. I appreciate that. But I want people laughing with us, not *at* us."

Jen stretched out on a couch and put her hands behind her head. "It's a little late to change the finale, Dawson," she said. "I don't think this cast could handle any more changes."

"I wasn't thinking of scrapping it entirely," Dawson began. "I just want to change something. But what that something is, I have to admit I—"

From onstage, someone began singing without accompaniment. It was "Silent Night."

Silent night, holy night
All is calm, all is bright

"Who is *that*?" Dawson asked, before Jen and Andie both shushed him. He knew his cast, and no one in his cast had that voice. Whoever was singing had a truly beautiful, obviously trained voice.

They all listened, transfixed, as the unseen singer finished the famous Christmas carol, letting the final notes linger in the air of the cavernous auditorium.

"I've got to see who it is," Dawson exclaimed, jumping to his feet. He was on his way to the stage before his friends could even get to their feet. He practically ran to the stage. "Who in my cast is singing like that?" he shouted.

The singer was there to greet him.

Sundae Ramone.

"No one in your cast, Dawson," Sundae said slyly. She stood at the edge of the stage, her hands on her hips. "Exactly no one."

Dawson's jaw dropped. "You sang that?"

Sundae smiled, then turned toward the empty auditorium again.

Silent night, holy night
All is calm, all is bright

Sundae stopped and looked at Dawson again, as a few dumbfounded members of the cast drifted into the auditorium. They'd heard her singing, too.

"I just love singing to an empty house," Sundae said. "The acoustics are so much better than with all those nasty human bodies to soak up the sound. On the other hand, empty seats can't give me the standing ovation I so richly deserve."

"Where did you learn to sing like that?" Dawson asked her softly, the wheels already beginning to turn in his head. Maybe, just maybe . . .

"N.Y.U. has a great training program. All I needed

was the right teacher. I sucked in *Oklahoma*, but I think I've improved a little since then," Sundae said smugly.

Dawson found himself at a loss for words.

"Satisfied, Dawson?" she asked, turning back to him. Then, without a further word, she walked away.

Chapter 8

Dawson sat back on his bed and brooded.

From the moment that he'd first heard Sundae singing "Silent Night" in the high school auditorium that afternoon, he'd been enraptured. In fact, for the rest of the rehearsal, try as he did to concentrate on what his cast was doing, he couldn't get her exquisite soprano voice out of his head.

At almost the same moment that he'd first heard her, he'd seen it in his mind's eye—the perfect change to the grand finale that he knew had to be made, but which he didn't know how to execute.

Now, even though it was nearly midnight, he was wide awake, his eyes open, but seeing something other than the late local news that was on his television screen.

Dawson saw it as if it were unfolding in front of

him. It was the night of Capeside Winter Follies. Arthur and Leonard were in the audience. The show was completely hokey, and they knew it. Everyone knew it. They'd close with "This Land Is Your Land." It would be over-the-top hokey, true. But the show didn't have to end there. Did it?

The line of singers would part in the middle, and the lights on the stage would dim, all except for a single spot focused downstage on a single singer. Sundae Ramone. She would sing "Silent Night" alone, a cappella, no piano, so achingly beautiful and spiritual that there would not be a dry eye in the house.

The song would end, the spot would go out, the curtain would drop, and everyone would remember that this was, above all, a Christmas pageant.

And the applause would begin.

Dawson pulled himself out of his reverie as the news switched to a promo for the sports report. Okay, it was too much to hope for, Dawson thought, that Arthur and Leonard would actually choose our show for Broadway. But at least Capeside would not have been completely embarrassed.

Dawson sighed. He once again saw Sundae Ramone turning around to him, that smug smile on her face, those patronizing words coming from her lips about how much she liked to sing in an empty auditorium.

"She knew exactly what I was thinking," Dawson told himself aloud, realizing once again how much she was rubbing it in, because there's no way she'll ever be in this show as long as he was directing it.

He idly looked at the television. The sports report had come on and was finishing up—the Celtics had won, the Bruins had lost. The weather followed. There was a chance of flurries overnight, as a low-pressure system barreling up the Atlantic coast passed far offshore to the east. Then, the next several days would be clear, cold, and dry. The long-range forecast was the same.

Dawson frowned. Not only did he still have a headache over the conclusion to his show, but it looked like there wasn't a prayer of there being a white Christmas. He was going to need help.

He went to his window and looked across the now mostly frozen creek. We'll be skating on it in a few days, he thought, if it stays cold. On the other side of the creek, the lights from Potter's B and B were clearly visible. Lights were on in Rooms 2 and 3, which was where Arthur and Leonard were staying.

And the light was on in Joey's room, too.

Dawson didn't hesitate. He picked up the phone and dialed. "Joey? It's me," he said, when she answered. "Wasn't there a time when Sandi Rudman—er, Sundae Ramone, went to Europe for the summer, and you had to baby-sit for her little sister?"

"Indeed there was, Dawson," Joey said. *"The Endless Summer*, with Serena Rudman. It was like *The Bad Seed* come to life. Only Serena had less charm. Sage Rudman asked me a few times this year. I said no, and I didn't care how much money she wanted to pay me."

"Perfect!" Dawson exclaimed. "You have a relationship with the family. I have a plan, Joey, and I need your help with it."

*   *   *

"Dawson, wake up!"

Dawson opened his eyes. Jen was shaking his arm. He looked at the clock. 9:15 A.M. "What is it?" he asked groggily.

"What is it? It's just the blizzard of the new century, that's what it is. Fourteen inches on the ground—and on Grams's roof, too, incidentally—and maybe another fourteen forecast for tonight. It's only flurries now, though. You can forget rehearsal today. And tomorrow too, if the plows don't get through."

Dawson was on his feet and bounded over to the window. A sea of white greeted him. "Whoa," he said. Excitement bubbled up in his stomach. "It looks like it did when I was a kid."

"You're still a kid," Jen pointed out. "Now, do you think you can come over and help shovel off Grams's roof? The snow's kind of wet and she's afraid the porch is going to collapse."

Within fifteen minutes, Dawson had wolfed down a quick breakfast and hurried across the yard to Grams's place. Grams's worry was not misplaced—heavy snow on a flat roof had caused more than one roof collapse in Capeside that Dawson could remember. His father was already on the roof, working. So were Pacey and Jack.

"Hello Mister Director!" Jack called down to him. "How awesome is this?"

"Very!" Dawson shouted back.

"There's a shovel against the garage. Come on up here and help us make some art."

Grams was standing behind the front storm door of her house, a look of pure gratitude on her face.

She waved a big hello to Dawson, and Dawson smiled at her.

Why couldn't all of life be this simple, he thought. It snowed too much, you assembled a bunch of guys, you climbed up on a roof, and you shoveled it off. You didn't have to be bright or talented or cute or anything. Just willing to do the work. So often he felt as if he got caught up in his own talent and ambition, either believing in it too strongly, or doubting its very existence.

He grabbed the shovel, then carefully climbed the ladder to the roof.

"Glad to see you, son," Mitch said, as he let a load of heavy, wet snow fly.

"I would have come sooner," Dawson said, a little sheepishly. "But I didn't—"

"Dawson, Dawson," Pacey said to him. "We told your dad to let you sleep. You're overworked as it is these days."

It didn't take more than an hour for the four of them, working cautiously, to get all the snow off the roof. If the snow actually started up again, they might have to do the job again tomorrow morning, but for the moment, the danger to Grams's roof was gone.

Rehearsal, though, was out of the question. Too many people wouldn't be able to make it. Pacey and Jack went home, and Mitch went back home, too. Jen, though, asked Dawson if he could hang out for a minute. She had a favor to ask of him, she said. She'd be right down.

Dawson sat down on the porch swing, wet

and tired, but oddly content, even with rehearsal canceled.

A moment later, Jen reappeared. She was carrying a small overnight bag. "Planning a trip?" Dawson asked her, wryly. "I hear extreme northern Canada is pleasant this time of year. Actually, it would probably look just like this."

"Dawson, could you give me a ride to the train station? Your dad's got four-wheel drive, the trains are running, and if we're not rehearsing, I want to go to New York to see my mother."

Dawson was shocked. Just a few days before, Jen had told him that she'd had a big fight with her mother and wasn't going to go home for Christmas at all. She was his stage manager. What was he going to do without her?

"But, Jen—"

"I'm not quitting the Follies. I'm just going to New York overnight to see my mother. And my father, if he happens to be around."

"Are you sure this is something you want to do?"

"Are you worried about me, Dawson, or are you worried about the Follies?"

"To be totally honest, both," Dawson admitted. "And I remember how much pain you were in when your mother was here—"

"Yeah, well, family can do that to you. Don't worry," Jen added. "I'll be fine. And I'll be back for tomorrow evening's rehearsal—that is, if there is a rehearsal tomorrow evening. I promise."

Dawson hesitated. "I just don't want to see you hurt, Jen."

"The thought is appreciated, Dawson. But we all get hurt, all the time, for all kinds of reasons. So, it's a simple question, and the next train to Boston and then New York leaves in an hour. Can you give me a ride to the train station? Yes, or no?"

Andie opened the front door. The delivery boy stood there, bundled up to his eyeballs, looking like Kenny from *South Park* in his gigantic parka.

"Delivery, Andie McPhee," he mumbled through his ski mask, barely understandable.

"I'm Andie McPhee," Andie said, puzzled. She wasn't expecting anything from anyone. And she marveled that anyone would try to deliver a package to her on a day like this, after so much snow had fallen. Dawson had canceled rehearsal, and so she had the afternoon to herself. She was spending it looking through a huge collection of college catalogues she'd amassed. Not that anything could touch Harvard. But no one would ever accuse her of not being thorough in her college selection process.

"You're Andie McPhee?" the delivery guy mumbled. "Be right back."

Andie shrugged as the guy made his way back down the path Jack had shoveled earlier that led from the street to their front door. He went into the back seat of his Explorer and took out a bouquet of flowers so large it obliterated the upper half of him as he headed back to Andie.

"Flowers for me?" Andie marveled. "Who are they from?"

"Card," the guy mumbled through his ski mask,

handing her the bouquet. He pointed. He was right. A card was perched between two beautiful purple flowers.

Andie took the card and read it.

Sweet spring flowers for Capeside's sweetest ventriloquist. Hockey players have hearts. Yours, Bill.

"Oh, that is so sweet!" Andie exclaimed. Then she got an idea. "Hey, are you in a hurry?"

"Yeah, I thought I'd head to the creek for a swim," the guy cracked.

Andie squinted at him. "Do I know you, whoever you are under there?"

"Nope."

"If I write a card, can you bring it back to the guy who sent these? I'll give you the address."

The delivery guy nodded.

"I'll be right back," Andie said. "Do you want to come in? Can I get you some hot chocolate or something?"

The guy shook his head.

Andie shrugged. "Okay, well, I'll hurry." She dashed upstairs, took out one of her personal note cards, and quickly wrote a thank you to Bill Curtson, saying how much the flowers meant to her and how seeing them really did make her think of her favorite time of year, spring. They must have cost him a fortune in the middle of winter. How thoughtful could one guy get?

"How should I sign it?" she mused, nibbling on the end of her pen. Finally, she wrote, *Warmly,*

Andie, sealed it, and brought it downstairs to the delivery guy.

"Do you think you could deliver it right away?" she asked. "How much will that cost?"

"Two thousand, give or take a few bucks for tax and tip."

Delivery Guy pulled off his ski mask and unwrapped the scarf that covered his mouth and chin.

Bill Curtson was sheepishly smiling at her. "Actually, it won't cost a thing to deliver it," he said, grinning. "That is, if it's okay for the guy whose name is on the envelope to open it right now."

Chapter 9

Dawson looked at his watch: 6:55 P.M. Rehearsal was starting at seven. His cast was already assembled backstage, going through a warm-up led by Pete McCutter, and Chester was busy warming up at the piano.

It was just seven days away now from the Winter Follies performance. Dawson had thought that there would be no way that they could get the rehearsal in because of the weather, but the weather report had been wrong. Instead of more snow, a warm front had forced its way up from the south, and temperatures has risen steadily through the night and day. The thermometer now stood at a balmy fifty degrees. There was running water everywhere from all the melting snow. In fact, it was so warm that before rehearsal, Pacey and Jack had been throwing around a night-glow Frisbee in the high school parking lot, dodging puddles.

But, even with the unusually warm weather, Dawson was feeling intensely frustrated. First of all, Joey had called him that afternoon to report that her intervention with Sundae Ramone—to try to get her over her animosity and into the cast of the show—so that she could sing "Silent Night" as part of the grand finale, had ended in abject failure.

"She says to tell you that even if the Secretary General of the United Nations asked her, she'd turn him down. That is, if you are still directing the play," Joey had reported. "On the other hand, if you resign and let her direct, you have a chance. But that's only if you agree not to come on opening night. In other words, the girl hates your guts."

Joey had gone on to say that she had even talked to Sage, to try to get the mother to convince the daughter to do it for the good of Capeside. But Sage hadn't shown much enthusiasm, either. Basically, there was no hope.

So much for my brilliant idea, Dawson thought. *I'm right back where I was—with the hokey-est ending to a Christmas show since* The Christmas that Almost Wasn't. *No. Worse.*

Joey had more news for Dawson. She'd warned him that Arthur and Leonard were going to be sending their wives to the evening's rehearsal, to scout the show and bring back a report to them.

Like the wives knew what was good simply by virtue of being married to producers, Dawson thought. One more thing to think about. Spectators with scorecards.

And there was one more thing—actually, it was the thing that concerned Dawson the most. Jen, who had promised him yet again right before he'd left her at the train station that she would be back in Capeside in time for rehearsal, still wasn't at the auditorium. Dawson himself had called the station, and the train from New York and then Boston had arrived right on schedule at four-thirty that afternoon.

But, apparently, Jen hadn't been a passenger on it.

"Don't worry, Dawson," Andie counseled him. "If Jen said she'd be back for rehearsal today, she's going to be back for rehearsal today. And if she's not, I'm sure it's for a good reason."

"You're not calling light and sound cues today, anyway, Dawson," Jack said. "Anything else, I can take over for her."

Dawson thanked him, but he still looked deeply concerned.

"I mean it, Dawson," Andie repeated. "Don't worry about things you can't control."

"How very Zen of you, Andie."

"Thank you."

Dawson opened a notebook to look at some notes from the last rehearsal when he felt a tap on his shoulder. Jen? He spun around.

Joey. For an instant, as much as he was anxious about Jen, he was flooded with relief just to see her face. That just seeing Joey could still do that to him made him both happy and sad at the same time.

Joey wasn't alone. With her were two absolutely beautiful young women who looked to be in their late twenties or early thirties. By the time he'd finished talking to Joey about Jen, he'd figured out who the women were. But he decided the smart thing to do was to feign ignorance.

"Um, Joey, are you going to introduce me to your friends?" he asked. "I can't say I've seen them in Capeside before."

Joey smiled. "Dawson, I want you to meet Charma Arthur, her husband is the celebrated theater producer." The woman with the gorgeous red hair smiled radiantly. "And Gwendolyn Leonard. Her husband is also a celebrated theater producer."

The one with the Winona Ryder haircut grinned. "Please call me Gwen, Dawson. Joey has told us all about you. We think it's just great that you're directing the Christmas show."

"All the directors in Hollywood are like, twenty years old or something," Charma added.

Gwen nodded. "Toast if you haven't made it by thirty."

"Good thing you're already getting into the game, ya know?" Charma concluded.

"Gee, that's . . . interesting," Dawson said. "We're truly pleased to have you here in Capeside. The only thing is, I ask that you don't mention to my cast who you are or why you're in town. I don't want to make them more nervous than they already are."

"Don't worry, Dawson," Charma said earnestly. "Our husbands are the ones here to see your show. They just wanted us to give them some advance word on how it's going. So they thought if we came, instead of them coming . . ."

Gwen nodded. "We could just be two really cute older sisters of kids in the cast or something. No one in your show will suspect a thing."

Dawson considered the situation. For a moment, he was tempted to ask them if two women who looked like they looked were sitting in the back of the theater taking notes, did they really think his cast would believe they were older sisters of cast members?

But he kept his mouth shut on the subject.

"Well, I hope that you enjoy our rehearsal," Dawson told them, trying to stay as confident as he could and rearrange his rehearsal plans at the same time. "We're just going to, er, just be doing some clean-up work today. You really can't judge the show by clean-up work. Jack, can you call places and get Pete McCutter on deck for his routine? Andie, let's start with you and Witty."

Andie, who was deep in conversation with Bill Curtson, heard her name called. Instantly, she was unpacking her ventriloquist's dummy and taking a seat on the edge of the stage. Meanwhile, Jack went backstage to quiet the cast down, and the two producers' wives took seats in the back of the auditorium.

Andie's act consisted of the dummy, Witty, giving Andie advice on love and dating during the Christmas season, and ended with the dummy asking Andie to skip Christmas dinner with her own family and come over to his bachelor apartment for Christmas dinner. When Andie refused, Witty kept improving the offer, suggesting that Andie would receive all kinds of presents—including a trip around the world with him—if she would merely accept.

She didn't even have to kiss him.

In the back of the room, Dawson heard Charma and Gwen laughing like Andie was the funniest thing they'd ever heard. When she and Witty took a bow, the women applauded.

Dawson relaxed a little. Gwen and Charma were having a good time. It looked like at least one thing was going well.

But what the heck had happened to his stage manager? Where was Jen?

"You what?" Dawson asked Gwen and Charma, scarcely believing his ears.

"Your cast was asking us questions, like who we were and where did we come from," Charma told Dawson, as the rehearsal was breaking up. "We didn't want to lie to anyone."

"You told them who you were?" Dawson swallowed hard. "But I specifically asked you—"

Joey came up behind Dawson. "Dawson, it's all right," she assured him. "You can't keep a secret in Capeside. How long did you think that you'd be able to hide it from the cast?"

"I didn't want to tell them until this weekend, at least," Dawson said, sighing. "My phone is going to be ringing off the hook." Just then, the Bowerses came out from backstage, walking right past Dawson, Joey, Charma, and Gwen. They looked at the wives of the Broadway producers as if they were seeing a divine revelation.

Happiness is two kinds of ice cream!

Suddenly, Serena Rudman's overblown soprano pierced the air from offstage. Clearly, she had heard that the wives of the producers were in the theater, and was doing her best to try to impress them.

"Joey, please do me a favor, go tell Serena that when rehearsal ends, like it did five minutes ago, she should go home and rest her voice," Dawson asked.

"Can I strangle her little neck while I'm at it? Consider that rhetorical." Joey bounded up onto the stage. Moments later, Dawson heard a loud protest from Serena, but at least the singing stopped.

"You know, Dawson, we had something else we wanted to ask you," Charma began.

Dawson steeled himself. What could it possibly be? The two women were looking at each other, and the looks on their faces were actually sheepish.

"Go ahead, tell him," Gwen urged.

"You tell him," Charma replied. "Or ask him. Whatever."

Gwen was actually blushing. "Well, we don't really know how to say this, so we'll just come right out and say it. The thing is, after watching rehearsal today, Charma and I decided we want to be in your show," she said.

"You *what*?"

"Capeside Winter Follies," Charma exulted. "It's just so charming. It should be a reality show on television, like *Survivor,* or something. I mean, it really shows the positive side of humans, don't you think?"

"It's better than *Survivor,*" Gwen agreed.

"Because it's not fake, it's totally real," Charma added. "Real people, real America. I grew up in Los Angeles. We never had snow at Christmas. We never had a Christmas pageant, either. And I always wanted to be in one."

"We came up here to go antiquing, but all the antique shops are closed until after New Year's," Gwen explained, the words tumbling out of her mouth in a rush. "And we would just love to be a part of what you're doing."

"So we were watching the acts and thinking, hey, we're in Capeside, we could be a part of this," Charma told Dawson.

"That is, if you'll have us." Gwen looked anxiously at Dawson. "But it has to be a surprise to Arthur and Leonard."

Dawson's head was spinning so fast he couldn't muster up a word.

"Because if they find out beforehand, it won't be a surprise," Charma said, as her friend nodded anxiously.

"You want to be a surprise addition to my show," Dawson repeated, trying to sort this through in his mind.

But in some ways, the decision was already made: he was not about to tell the wives of Arthur and Leonard that they couldn't be in the Winter Follies. The mayor would drum him and his family out of Capeside.

Worse, Dawson realized, the cast already knew that Arthur and Leonard were in town. If the producers turned down the Winter Follies as their big Broadway seasonal musical, an event that Dawson figured was a one hundred percent certainty, the cast would blame Dawson if he hadn't allowed their wives to be in the show. But the show was running long already. How and where could he fit them in? What was their talent? Wouldn't it take something major away from the whole idea of the Follies?

"We'll blend in, honest," Gwen said earnestly.

"You don't have to worry, Dawson," Charma added. "We're both professional performers. I used to work at Harrah's in Las Vegas. That's how I met Arthur."

"And I met Leonard the same way," Gwen said.

Oh my God, Dawson thought. They used to be showgirls in Vegas.

"We were the lead singers in the lounge band. Charma, Gwen, and Idle Rich?"

"She used to be married to Idle Rich," Charma confided to Dawson. "But she doesn't talk about that much. It upsets Leonard. The girl can sing, though."

To emphasize her friend's point, Gwen did a few lines of an old Fleetwood Mac classic on the spot. Charma added a line of harmony.

They didn't sound bad at all.

"So, we were thinking that we could do a rocked-out version of something like 'White Christmas,' " Gwen said. "Do you think your piano player can handle that? Otherwise, I can play it, too."

"Uh, let me give it some thought," Dawson said to them. "The order of the show is pretty well put together. But why don't I call you at the B and B in the morning? And if it's going to work out, I can give you our rehearsal schedule."

"Thanks, Dawson." Charma put out her hand, and Dawson took it. "It means a lot to me and Gwen. And most of all, I'm sure it's going to mean a lot to our husbands."

Chapter 10

*"D*awson?"

Dawson had worked for two hours doing prep and clean-up work at his parents' restaurant after rehearsal, but then begged off, saying that he was too tired. He'd come straight home and was about to let himself into his house when he heard the female voice behind him.

But he didn't recognize it. He squinted into the darkness to see who was calling to him. A girl stepped out of the shadows.

Sundae Ramone.

"What brings you to my corner of Capeside?" Dawson asked her. "After midnight? Does it involve fangs and blood sucking?"

"I deserved that," Sundae said softly.

"Good, we're in agreement about something. My midnight is complete."

"Look Dawson, I was a jerk. I came to apologize to you. Can I come in, please?"

"Sure," Dawson said, by reflex. He was bone-tired. Jen hadn't shown up at rehearsal. He was going to have to deal with Arthur and Leonard's wives in his show, now. Frankly, Sundae was the last thing on his mind.

He led her into the kitchen.

"This won't take long, Dawson, I promise. I know you must be really wiped out from directing. I just want to say that I was a complete and total butt-hole about being in the Follies. And how I conducted myself as stage manager was reprehensible."

"Again we agree," Dawson said.

She stopped for a moment, biting her lower lip. "That's right. Reprehensible. That's the right word. I sucked."

"Sandi—Sundae, it's okay," Dawson told her. "Actually, I really do appreciate your coming out here to tell me that."

"Because I didn't want you to get the wrong idea about me, Dawson," Sundae said. Her voice dropped to a conspiratorial tone. "The thing is— don't tell anyone this, *please*—they changed my medication right before I came home from N.Y.U. It was getting me all weird. So I went back to Prozac yesterday. *Please*, don't tell anyone."

Guilt washed over Dawson immediately. He hadn't known she was having psychological problems so serious she needed Prozac. That really did explain everything.

"A director has to be willing to accept the confidences of his cast," Dawson told her earnestly. "Thank you for telling me."

"So does that mean I can be stage manager again?" Sundae asked. "I'll do anything you ask, the way that you want it."

Dawson hesitated. Jen wasn't back. What if she didn't come back from New York at all? He'd need a stage manager, preferably one who knew what she was doing. The show was getting more and more complicated by the minute.

"Frankly, that would be a lifesaver," Dawson admitted.

"Wonderful! And I truly do not mind doing double duty," Sundae added. "I can sing one number in your show and stage manage the rest of it, too. That's how grateful I am that you're giving me a second chance."

"To be honest, Sundae, I haven't been able to get your voice out of my head, since I heard you singing that day in the auditorium."

"I worked really hard this last semester with my vocal coach at N.Y.U.," Sundae said. "Is there something in particular you'd like me to sing at the Follies? Because all you have to do is ask."

"I was thinking about—" Dawson stopped.

He'd suddenly figured out exactly what Sundae was doing on his doorstep at a few minutes after midnight, on this particular night. He saw it all in his mind's eye: little Serena coming out of rehearsal, telling her mother Sage all about the big Broadway producers who were going to be coming to see the Capeside Winter Follies.

As soon as Sage got home, she'd told Sundae,

Dawson realized. And as soon as Sundae could figure out what her excuse could be, she came to see me. All she really wants is to be in the show so that she can be seen by Arthur and Leonard.

"Now that I think about it more carefully," Dawson began, "I'd like to put you in charge of the bake sale and blind auction. You know, in some ways, it's the most important event of the evening. The Winter Follies comes and goes, but the good that we'll be doing with that sale can go on for a long time. I'm sure you won't have time to participate in any other way with all that responsibility."

Sundae was stunned. "You're kidding," she stammered.

"No, I'm completely serious. In fact, I really appreciate your willingness to come back and help out like this, Sundae. I misjudged you."

"But that's not what I had in mind," Sundae replied, the color rising in her cheeks. "Okay, you might not want me to be your stage manager again, I can understand that. But I'm the best voice you've got in the whole town. And you know that."

"Was there anything else?" Dawson asked.

"You can't afford to not have me in the show!"

Dawson folded his arms. "You do have the best voice in this town. But that still doesn't mean I have to put you in the Follies. You are, in my opinion, not Capeside Christmas Follies material. And you're not in the show."

Tick, tick, tick, on Dawson's bedroom window. At first, Dawson thought it was the tick of sleet against the glass. But it didn't go away, the way sleet usually did when it changed to snow or rain.

Tick, tick, tick. Tick, tick, tick.

He opened his eyes. The first thing he saw was his clock: 5:15 A.M.

The next thing he saw was Jen, at his bedroom window, bundled up in a winter coat, tapping on the glass with her fingernails.

Dawson jumped out of bed, went to the window, and let her in, like he had done for Joey at the same window a thousand times. "Jen, are you okay?" he asked, looking at her closely.

Jen grimaced.

"As okay as you could be if you had the experience of the last six hours that I've had. I thought there was a constitutional amendment against cruel and unusual punishment." She sat on his bed and blew her nose. "Sorry for the early morning wake-up call."

"Forget about that. What happened?"

"You've heard of *Nightmare on Elm Street*? This was *Nightmare of the Broken Down Bus.*"

"Bad, huh?"

"Worse than that. We had a horrible ice storm and I hear another storm's moving this way." Jen shivered. "I was with my mother until about six hours ago. I missed the last train out, but I wasn't too worried, because I thought that the snow and ice would have canceled rehearsal."

"We rehearsed."

"Dawson, I am so sorry. I made a bad mistake in judgment. I definitely should have called you."

"If you missed the last train, how'd you get here?"

Jen reached into her pocket and took out a tattered bus ticket. "Greyhound. Leave the driving to us. You'd be amazed at who takes the all-night bus from New York to Boston. Then the heater broke. Then there was a mechanical difficulty. We sat. We froze. Need I say more?"

"What about Boston to here?"

"Taxi. Thanks, Mom," Jen said. "At least she paid for it." Jen's teeth chattered. "I'm still freezing."

Dawson sat next to her and draped a blanket around her shoulders. "I'm sorry you had such a lousy trip."

"I went home. I saw my mother. For exactly forty minutes the day I got there, before she had to go to some testimonial dinner for someone I never heard of at the Parker-Meridien Hotel. Then, the next day, she took me on her favorite outing. Shopping. I don't think we exchanged more than ten sentences and dropped roughly three thou at Saks at the same time. We get along, but sometimes I think we just don't have much to say to each other." Jen shivered.

Instead of speaking, Dawson gently pulled her close. She leaned against him. "Next time I'm really going to try to get through to her," she murmured.

Dawson nodded, and held her.

Chapter 11

"Head up, head up, head up!" Bill instructed Andie, as she gingerly skated her way across the rink, an oversize Boston Bruins hockey jersey over her sweater, an actual hockey stick in her hands.

"How can I keep my head up and see the puck at the same time?" she protested. "And this jersey weighs seven tons."

"Forget the uni. Feel the puck," Bill responded. "On your stick." He skated backward just in front of her.

"I am feeling the puck. Slipping away! Who invented this insane game, anyway?"

"Some guy who wanted to torture you, I guess," Bill said, laughing. "But you're doing great."

"Really? Thanks." At that moment the hockey puck, which she'd been stick-handling fairly well for the past fifty feet, slipped away from her stick and against the side boards of the rink, where it came to a stop.

"Chase it!" Bill instructed, laughing.

"You chase it, you're the hockey player."

Bill raised his right arm and gave a sharp whistle. "Penalty," he intoned, in the metallic voice of a public-address announcer. "Unsportsmanlike conduct, giving her hockey instructor the verbal business without adequate provocation, called on McPhee of Capeside. To the penalty box, for two minutes. Now!"

The Saturday afternoon before the Capeside Winter Follies show, Dawson had given the cast the entire day off. There would be a full run that night, with light and sound cues, but this Saturday afternoon he, Jack, and Jen were busy "dry" teching the Follies show without the actors. They were setting light and sound levels, figuring out where to place lights, and the like.

Andie knew that they had arrived at the high school auditorium before nine that morning, and they didn't expect any actors to arrive until seven that night. She'd asked Dawson if she could help out, but he'd refused. "Dry tech is a scary thing, Andie," he'd said. "Stay far away from the theater if you have any sense."

So Bill had invited Andie for a hockey lesson at the rink in Falmouth. Though on a normal Saturday afternoon the rink was packed, there was a time between two and two-thirty when it was not in use. Bill had used his friendship with the owner to allow him to give Andie a hockey lesson during this downtime.

"So let me ask you, Mr. Hockey Coach," Andie began. "What if I don't go into the penalty box?"

"You get suspended."

"Suspend McPhee? Never," she joked. "I'm much too valuable to the team."

Bill took a few quick steps with his skates, zoomed over toward the puck that rested against the near boards, caught it neatly with his stick, and skated quickly across the ice.

"The 'i' in Capeside Motors," he called to Andie. Then, he drew back his stick and let fly with an amazingly fast slap shot.

It literally hit the dot above the "i" in the Capeside Motors advertisement that had been painted on the far boards.

"Amazing!" Andie exclaimed. "How did you do that?"

"Well, I just—"

"Nice shot, Bill," said a disembodied voice over the public-address system. "But you and your friend are going to have to clear the ice so that we can get the afternoon session started."

Bill waved his hand above his head, showing that he understood, then turned to Andie. "You just got a reprieve on your penalty."

"But Mister Referee, I was ready to serve it."

"Why don't you serve it by having hot chocolate with me? We don't have to be at rehearsal for hours. I can't guarantee it'll take less than two minutes, though. You'll have to take your chances."

Twenty minutes later, Andie and Bill were sitting in the snack bar of the ice rink, steaming cups of hot chocolate before them. The ice was already crowded with recreational skaters, and Christmas carols were playing over the rink sound system.

"So," Bill said. "I'm here drinking hot chocolate with the most beautiful girl at Capeside High. And I just taught her how to stick-handle. Please don't wake me up, I'm loving this dream too much."

Andie blushed. "You don't really think that."

Bill frowned. "Yeah, I do. Why else would I say it?"

She shrugged and stared into her hot chocolate.

"I really did dream this, you know," he said softly. "Maybe a thousand times."

She looked up at him. "I'm flattered. And . . . I don't really know why you like me. Not that I'm not likeable. I mean, sometimes I can be extremely personable. But by an objective measure there are cuter girls at Capeside High than me, and—"

He reached for her hand to interrupt her. "I know what I see. Maybe I just see better than some other people."

She gazed at him. "I thought all hockey players had no teeth and an overload of testosterone. I'm glad you proved me wrong."

"I'm pretty sure I'm up there on the testosterone thing," Bill said.

"Right. Of course you are. I didn't mean that the way it sounded. I mean—"

Her words were cut off when Bill gently kissed her. And, though they were in a public place, she kissed him gently back.

"Whoa. Nothing wrong with testosterone," she said shakily, when the kiss was over.

"I dreamed about doing that, too. For a long, long time. Only the real thing was even better than my dreams."

She smiled radiantly. Suddenly, she felt so happy. How could she not have seen what a great guy he was? He wasn't stupid at all, he was just so into hockey that his path had never crossed Pacey's. Pacey had completely misjudged Bill.

"Okay, right at this moment, I happen to feel ridiculously happy," Andie announced.

"Me, too." Bill hesitated. "I think there's something I need to tell you."

Andie winced and tried to comically cover the dread that overtook her. "You're gay, you've got a boyfriend, you've got a girlfriend, you've got both, you're moving to Moscow, work with me here."

"Not Moscow," Bill said. "And not moving." He took a thoughtful sip of his hot chocolate.

"There's a girlfriend, then?"

"No."

"I don't understand."

Bill looked sheepish. "This is really weird, ya know? Because I always thought you were one of those unapproachable girls at school. Hanging with a brain like Joey Potter and junior film genius Dawson. Why would you even notice someone like me?"

"In case you haven't noticed, the jocks basically rule in high school," Andie pointed out. "That means you."

"I guess maybe I've always admired people who can do things I can't do."

"Bill? Why don't you tell me what you want to say?"

"I'm trying, this isn't easy."

"Just say it," Andie sighed. "Because this is making me insane."

"Well, the thing is, I'm not going to be in Capeside after New Year's."

Andie pulled her hands out of his. "I thought you just told me you aren't moving."

"I'm not."

"But—"

"A lot of hockey players—good ones, anyway—during their junior and senior years of high school, they go to another place to live so they can play on a certain team and work with a certain coach. I've been invited by a pretty famous amateur team to come to Grand Rapids, Michigan, to play for them for the rest of the season."

"Grand Rapids," Andie repeated, a little numb. "Grand Rapids, Michigan."

"I'll be living with a family there whose kid is on the same team. We'll go to high school together, my family pays his family a set amount for me for room and board, et cetera, et cetera."

He noticed Andie's downcast face. "It's not forever."

"It's not forever? Then what is it?" Andie asked, the color rising in her cheeks. "You're good. No, you're great. And you really got me to like you."

"Because I really like you, too." He looked bewildered.

"So what's going to happen?" she asked. She

heard her voice rising with anxiety, but she didn't care. "You go to Michigan, and then some other team sees you, and you go to Colorado or to Canada, and you're there for senior year, and then you get picked by some pro team, the Boston Whoevers or the Montreal Whatevers, and the next time I see you is on ESPN?"

"It isn't like that," Bill told her. "It won't be."

Andie stood up. "Maybe it won't be. But maybe it will be. I've been hurt too many times to take that chance. I'm sorry, but I'm not willing to let it happen again."

Without another word, she picked up her pocketbook and walked away.

The mayor picked up his wineglass and held it in his right hand. "In the presence of such august company, I want to propose a toast on behalf of the people of Capeside," he intoned.

"Hear, hear," Gwen seconded. "Shaddup, everyone. Listen to the mayor."

It was late that afternoon. Dawson and his crew at the theater had actually finished their dry tech at about four o'clock, much earlier than they had anticipated. It was a good thing, too. Because the mayor had shown up at the auditorium right when they were finishing, announcing that he had arranged for a catered dinner at Potter's B and B. Featured guests? Producers Arthur and Leonard. The mayor. And Dawson himself.

There was no time for Dawson to protest. The dinner was going to start at five o'clock and be over by six-thirty, in time for Dawson to get back to the auditorium for his dress rehearsal with the cast. Catering had been done by Gale and Mitch—they were in the kitchen when Dawson had arrived with the mayor.

It was a small group for dinner. Dawson, Joey, Bessie, the mayor, the two producers from New York, and their wives Gwen and Charma. Arthur and Leonard had been very kind to Dawson, marveling more than once that such a young guy had been put in charge of the show.

Before the mayor could proceed with his toast, Arthur stood up. "Lippy, sit down," he told the mayor. "Or else I'll tell everyone here that your nickname at Dartmouth was Lippy."

Everyone laughed, including the mayor, who yielded the floor to his college buddy.

"I just wanted to say how happy my partner and I are to be in Capeside." He held his glass high. "And to propose a toast to our hostesses for the week, Joey Potter and her sister Bessie. Anyone who can put up with four obnoxious New Yorkers for a week deserves a medal."

"Hear, hear," the mayor chortled.

"And also, though we haven't seen the show yet, I want to propose a toast to young Dawson," Arthur said. "Our wives have scouted your show and have brought back just the most glowing reports. I've learned from experience that you don't get glowing reports on a show unless it glows. So, while we won't get to see it until opening night, I have to tell you all that the chances for Capeside Winter Follies to be on Broadway next year are very, very good."

Gwen caught Dawson's eye and winked.

"Very good," Leonard said, looking directly at Dawson.

"To the director!" the mayor added. All the adults lifted their glasses and drank, while Dawson looked on, slightly shell-shocked. Broadway? Next season? Was it really possible?

No. No way. Dawson had known it was ludicrous all along. But still . . .

"I'm sure Dawson has a few words he'd like to say," the mayor prompted.

Dawson stood up, his mind a complete blank. "Well, I'd just like to say that, er, we're going to do the best Winter Follies that we can, that everyone has worked hard, and that it's a real honor for Capeside and for me to have you here for our show." His eyes lit on Gwen and Charma. "And also to have Gwen and Charma here. They add a lot to everything."

Joey nudged him in the arm, and motioned with her chin toward the kitchen.

"Excuse me," Dawson said quickly. "I need to go prepare for rehearsal. I'm sure you understand." He went into the kitchen; Joey quickly followed.

"What is up with that Gwen wink thing?" Joey asked. "Are you flirting with a married woman, one with an expensive and highly unattractive bleach job, I might add? Not that I care. But it is kind of tacky."

"The wink was about the show, Joey. Trust me."

The only person Dawson had told about his big plan for putting Gwen and Charma in the show, as well as his planning for the finale of the finale, was Jen. He hadn't rehearsed any of it, just simply took it on faith that it would work out. And, as sorely tempted as he was to explain things to Joey now, he kept his mouth shut.

"You're not going to tell me?" Joey asked.

"I'd rather surprise you."

Joey nodded. "You know what is bizarre? I really think that Arthur and Leonard are serious."

"I was there, Joey. I heard it. I can't believe it, but I heard it."

"When you first told me about them coming, I have to admit that I thought the whole thing was kind of a joke. That Capeside was just going to be a laughingstock for these big producers from New York. But this is for real."

"You have to admit, it seems impossible."

"Impossibly impossible. But that has never stopped you before, Dawson Leery. I just have to say that everyone is really impressed by how you're handling things. And I know that I can get weird around Christmas—no, I know that I *am* weird around Christmas. But you can count on me to help you any way I can."

She took his hand. "I mean it," she repeated. "You can count on me."

All Dawson could think was: once again, my hand's in Joey Potter's.

Chapter 12

"This is your five-minute call before final dress, ladies!" Jen called into the art classroom, which was serving as one of the women's dressing rooms. "Places in five, please." She ducked out again to go yell the same thing into the other dressing rooms, better known as the science lab and two English classrooms.

On her way back to the stage, she ran into Andie, eyes closed, dancing in place.

Jen peered at her. "Are you okay?"

Andie opened her eyes but kept dancing. "I just got a better idea for the combination step I gave them during the finale. Is it still snowing outside?"

"Yes," Jen said. "You're not actually thinking that there's time to change anything, are you?"

"I just want it to look totally professional."

Jen groaned inwardly. She couldn't believe that her friends were taking the Arthur and Leonard thing so seriously. She patted Andie's arm. "It's great the way it is, Andie."

"You think?"

"Without a doubt."

As Jen hurried off to get her headset, through which she'd call the technical cues for the show, she noticed Bill approaching Andie. He began to speak, but Andie turned on her heel and ran past Jen toward the ladies' room, obviously really upset.

Jen hesitated. Andie had already told her about Bill leaving for Michigan, and she knew how devastated Andie was about it. But did she really have time to go see if Andie was all right? She checked her watch. Oh, so what if the dress rehearsal started five minutes late. Andie was more important.

She swung through the ladies' room door. Andie was leaning against the wall, crying. "Don't look at me," Andie sobbed. "I look like a duck when I cry."

"You know, you're right," Jen agreed. "You kind of do."

That made Andie laugh in spite of her misery. Jen fished a tissue out of her pocket and handed it over. "I just wanted to say that I know how you feel."

Andie blew her nose. "You do?"

"A guy is crazy about you. He pursues you. You're not into him and you're never going to be into him. And then one day it almost takes you by surprise, because he's all you can think about. He's under your skin, in your heart, in the air you breathe."

Andie nodded.

"And then he announces that he's leaving for wherever. It doesn't matter. All that matters is that he made you love him and now he's leaving and this is the first you've ever heard about it."

Andie nodded again, wiping her eyes.

"Well, my sad little tale is named Henry. Yours is named Bill."

"Love stinks, Jen. It really does." She blew her nose again. "Anyway, thanks for coming in here to tell me that."

"You're welcome. Now get your butt backstage while I go find my headset."

She had almost made it backstage when someone grabbed her arm. She swung around. Mr. Bowers was clutching her denim shirt.

"Everything okay, Mr. Bowers?"

He shook his head violently and pointed to his throat.

"Can you breathe?" she asked quickly.

He nodded vigorously and stabbed his finger toward his throat again.

"I'm sorry, Mr. Bowers, but I don't have time for twenty questions. What seems to be the problem?"

At that moment, Elmo Beard tiptoed up behind Mr. Bowers, blew up a paper bag and popped it near his ear.

"Are you insane?" Jen shrieked.

Strangely enough, Mr. Bowers smiled and exhaled with relief. "Thanks, old friend," he told Elmo. "I owe you one." He toddled back toward his dressing room.

"I am totally lost here," Jen said.

"He suffers from debilitating stage fright," Mr. Beard explained. "It gives him psychosomatic laryngitis every year at dress rehearsal. And every year, I scare him out of it and he's perfectly fine again."

"Oh. Great. Well, thanks." Jen dashed for the theater door. Dawson must be going crazy wondering where she was.

"Shall I take my seat at the piano now?" Mr. Pinkley asked Jen as she grabbed her earphones and put them on. "Or would you rather that I make an entrance and bow to the applause as I'll do tomorrow night?"

"You bow to the applause?" Jen echoed. "What if they don't applaud, Mr. Pinkley?"

"Oh, it works out just fine every year. My wife starts it, you see."

"Ah. Well, we'll skip that part tonight. You can go to the piano."

"All righty, then. But I hear there's a bad ice storm on the way. Hope we have an audience."

"We will," Jen replied firmly, and crossed her fingers.

Jen turned her headset on. She knew Dawson was sitting near the back of the auditorium, wearing another headset so that they could communicate with each other.

"Dawson?"

"Jen?"

"Sorry. I was, as they say, unavoidably detained," Jen said into her headset. "Do you want me to call places?"

"I want you to call me a cab so I can make a

smooth exit, actually," Dawson said. "Bethany and Bruce Bowers are standing in the aisle not ten feet from me, even as we speak, ready to come to blows."

"What's up? I just saw him get over an awful case of stage fright."

"It seems the ever popular Sundae left a message on their phone saying that, in the artistic opinion of the entire cast, he should play Juliet and his wife should play Romeo. He wants to drop out of the show. She wants the show to go on. I think they're about to duke it out."

"If they do, she'll win," Jen predicted.

"Look, tell everyone to get into place and I'll deal with this," Dawson said wearily. "Somehow. Along with the lousy weather. And everything else."

"You got it."

Jen headed down the hallway toward the make-shift dressing rooms. Pacey hurried over to her. "It seems we have a situation."

"Why do I so dislike the sound of that?"

"You're going to dislike it even more when you hear what it is. Andie can't find Witty."

"You're telling me the girl lost her dummy?"

"It seems I am. She's marched into every dressing room, pushing aside nearly naked male flesh in her single-minded pursuit of a little wooden man. He appears to have left the premises."

"He can't have 'left the premises,' Pacey. He can't walk. He's a dummy."

Pacey winced. "That's so politically incorrect. Please refer to him as consciousness-challenged."

"Someone took my dummy!" Andie screeched as

she marched down the hall toward them. "Someone will pay!"

"Jen, I got a hole in my tights," Serena whined, tugging on Jen's hand. "And I can't find my cherry lip gloss."

Jen threw her hands in the air. "Places! Do the best you can, people. The dress rehearsal must go on."

Before anyone else could tell her their latest crisis, she disappeared backstage.

Dawson's head pounded as he watched the cast marching in time onstage as they sang "Capeside Is Your Town" to the tune of "This Land Is Your Land."

Capeside is your town
Capeside is my town
From White's Hardware Store
To our real great downtown!

No matter how many times Dawson heard his cast perform it, it never became any less painful. But he couldn't change it now. The show was what it was. And it wasn't like he took the presence of Arthur and Leonard seriously. Except that they'd be judging his work as a director. Except that they were really, really important producers who, rumor had it, were about to delve into film as well as theater.

Except that they would watch the Capeside Winter Follies and then probably ban him from show business for life.

The dress rehearsal had been a total disaster. Pretty much everything that could go wrong, had gone wrong.

Costumes and cues were missed. Lyrics and dance steps forgotten. Bruce Bowers had interrupted his Romeo soliloquy to demand that anyone who had a problem with his performance should be man or woman enough to confront him directly, as in behind the school, after the rehearsal.

Visions of various tropical paradises had danced through Dawson's head. At that moment, Capeside was the very last place on the planet he wanted to be.

"Merry Christmas, everybody!" the cast called out as they flung their hands in the air for their big finish. Ellen Beard's hand smacked Bethany Bowers in the face by mistake.

After that, the cast waited, peering out into the darkened house for directions on what to do next. "That was great, everyone, lots of heart!" Dawson called to them.

People murmured. They knew what a disaster it had been.

"I'm not saying we were without some minor and easily fixable problems," Dawson acknowledged. "But there is a famous saying in the theater: bad dress rehearsal, great show."

"Excuse me, excuse me!" Serena bellowed from stage front and center, where she managed to place herself no matter where anyone told her to stand.

"House lights please, Jen," Dawson called. As the house lights went on, Dawson turned back to Serena. "Yes?"

"Are we going to practice our curtain calls now?" the girl asked.

"We'll go over that tomorrow an hour before the show," Dawson told her. "It'll be very simple. Everyone will join hands and bow while Mr. Pinkley plays "Jingle Bells" on the piano. Serena put her hands on her hips. "But that's not *fair*. Why does everyone get the same bow?"

"Because I said so and I am the director. To continue, artificial snow will float down on you as you bow."

"Check on the artificial snow!" Jack called from the catwalk above them. "You don't want it now, do you?"

"Save it for tomorrow Jack, thanks," Dawson responded.

"Don't need no artificial snow," a cast member dolefully pointed out. "There's gonna be snow all night and some bad ice. Doubt if anyone will come, anyway." The cast murmured, worried.

Dawson responded, "Of course they'll come. They always have." *But not to a show directed by me,* his brain couldn't help reminding him. "Thanks, everyone. Super job."

The cast half-heartedly applauded for themselves and began to drift offstage. Pacey plopped down in the seat next to Dawson. "Okay, so we both know the show bites."

"Don't feel you have to mince words on my account, Pacey," Dawson replied dryly.

"You are taking this way too seriously, my man." Pacey linked his fingers together behind his neck. "Chill out, that's my advice. Variety isn't covering your opening."

"No. Two famous theater producers are."

"Speaking of which . . ." Pacey looked behind him toward the back of the house, then back at Dawson. "Where are the infinitely better-looking halves of the famous theatrical producers' equation?"

"Not here."

"Yes, that was apparent," Pacey said. "But I distinctly recall your confiding in me that Gwen and Charma wanted to be in the show. And I distinctly noticed they were not in it."

"How keenly observant of you, Pacey."

"So, you didn't put them in the show, then?"

Dawson clapped Pacey on the back. "Watch and see, buddy. Watch and see."

"Meaning you did put them in the show? Give me something to work with, here."

Jen had joined them and overheard the last part of their conversation. She laughed and traded looks with Dawson.

"Just what are you two cooking up?" Pacey asked.

"A surprise," Jen replied. "Wait and see."

"Thank you for enlightening me," Pacey said. "It's all so much clearer now."

"Let me just put it this way," Jen began. "If it works, Dawson will be King of the Follies tomorrow night. And if it doesn't, we can take up a collection to help him sneak out of town."

"And if there's no audience due to the storm," Pacey put in helpfully, "all of this won't matter anyway."

Chapter 13

"**I** must have been out of my mind," Dawson told his reflection, as he stood before his dresser mirror. "In two hours, the Capeside Winter Follies will begin, and I will be humiliated in front of the entire town, not to mention two of the top theatrical producers in the world. That is, if we have *any* audience whatsoever."

"Decent line delivery, however, using the mirror to get in your expository state of mind borders on the cheesy, don't you think?"

Dawson turned around, where Joey stood in the doorway, looking like her usual adorable Joey self.

"Hello to you, too," Dawson said. "And thank you for those words of support. How long were you standing there?"

"Long enough. I would have used your window,

for old time's sake, but it's frozen shut! Cheer up, I know at least Bessie is coming," said Joey. Dawson groaned.

"I just stopped by to mention that I am suddenly absolutely terrified at the thought of doing some truly lame comedy routine with Pacey," said Joey. "I'd welcome words of support, but it sounds like you don't have any to spare."

"You'll be great, Joey," he assured her. "Your act with Pacey really is funny."

She looked dubious. "Really?"

"Really."

She flashed a disarming grin. "Well then, you really did direct a heck of a Follies."

"Kindness is your long suit, Joey."

"Not really, Dawson. Not always, anyway. And I'm not being kind now. I'm telling you the truth. I really am proud of you."

To Dawson's surprise, a lump formed in his throat. "Thanks, Joey."

"You're welcome. Well, now that we've formed our own mutual admiration society, shall we go face our public?"

"Sure." He flipped off the light and grabbed his parka. "Just one other thing."

"Which is?"

"We didn't form a mutual admiration society, Joey. It's always been there."

Dawson wouldn't open his eyes. He *heard* rustling. He heard conversation. There *was* an audience. The question was, How big?

132

"Break a leg, honey," Gale whispered to Dawson, kissing his cheek. Dawson looked. The house was packed. Even though it was the coldest day of the year, Capeside had come through. Dawson grinned. Then he realized that now he had to wow the town. Mr. Pinkley bowed to the audience's smatter of applause, then took his seat at the piano.

"Thanks, Mom," said Dawson. "I'm still sorry that you and Dad aren't in the show."

"There's always next year, son," Mitch said, from the seat next to his mother. He checked his watch. "Shouldn't the house lights be going down already? There isn't any problem, is there?"

"I'm sure Jen's on top of it," Dawson said with false bravado. At the moment, he wasn't sure of anything at all. He craned his neck to check out Leonard and Arthur, who sat in their reserved seats, fifth row center, right next to the mayor and his wife. People in the audience were looking at them and whispering. Evidently everyone in Capeside knew who they were and why they were there. The knowledge just made Dawson feel even more sick than he had before.

A woman with long black hair held back by a too-large red sequined bow, stopped in the aisle, midway to the stage. She wore Spandex tiger-print Capri pants with dangerously high heels, and a fake fur jacket dyed purple. She peered at the ticket in her hand, then peered at the woman in the seat on the end.

"Excuse me. I said excuse me, but you're in my seat!" she screeched loudly, her voice so abrasive that it cut through the excited murmurs in the theater.

The woman in her seat ignored her.

The woman in the aisle tapped her on the shoulder. "Yo, you deaf? Then read my lips. Get your butt out of my seat!"

Now, everyone was turned toward the spectacle of the red-faced woman in the aisle. The woman who was allegedly in the other woman's seat stood up, shaking platinum blond curls off her heavily made-up face. "You got a lotta nerve, Missy."

"And you gotta lotta butt. Jeez, who hit you with the ugly stick?"

"Yeah? Look whose talking, Missy!" the blonde sputtered.

"Plus which, the name is Roxy, not Missy. Now move your caboose outta my seat!" She brandished her ticket stub in the other woman's face.

"Shouldn't you do something, Dawson?" Gale whispered to her son.

He shook his head no, and just sat there.

"You wanna fight, you witch, I'll give you a fight!" The dark-haired woman bellowed. "I'll snatch you bald-headed!"

"Dawson, if you don't do something about this, I will," Mitch insisted.

"Dad, please." Something about the look on Dawson's face kept Mitch in his seat.

"Yeah, you and what army?" the blonde taunted.

"Do I need to call security or what?" the other woman huffed.

The blonde moved into the aisle. "You don't exactly reek of Christmas spirit. You just reek!"

"Oh yeah? I'll deck more than your halls!"

To the horror of the spellbound audience, the two women grabbed at each other's hair . . . all of which came off in their hands.

It was Gwen and Charma, who grinned broadly and waved their wigs to the still-shocked audience. "Welcome, welcome, welcome, this ain't your grandma's Follies, folks!" they both yelled. Then they bounded up onto the stage, as the curtains opened, the lights dimmed, and they joined the assembled cast for the opening number, "Holly Jolly Follies."

When the number finished, the audience applauded so hard, the sound was deafening.

"You really had me going there, Dawson," Gale told her son. "Very nervy opening." She patted his hand. "I like that quality in a son."

When the first act finished, Pacey took center stage and announced that the bake sale and blind auction was now taking place in the gym.

"All the money raised will go toward the Capeside Cares Foundation," Pacey explained. "So go eat six or seven desserts, bid high and bid often."

The house lights came up to signal intermission, and the crowd began to move from their seats.

"Dawson!" the mayor called, hurrying over to him. "Wonderful opening, son. Just wonderful. You had me going there, I'll admit." He cocked his head toward Arthur and Leonard, who hadn't moved from their seats. "I wish you could have seen the look on the boys' faces when their wives started screaming at each other in those awful wigs and outfits."

"Did they love it or hate it?" Dawson ventured.

"You wowed them, son! How the heck did you and Gwen and Charma keep it from them, that's what I want to know."

"We were highly motivated," Dawson explained.

The mayor chuckled. "Well, if the second act is as boffo as the first act, son, I'm naming you the new permanent director of the Capeside Winter Follies!"

Halfway through the second act, Dawson could feel his shoulders begin to relax. The show was going really well. In fact, nothing major had gone wrong. Serena had belted out her song like a little pro. Andie and Witty were a major hit. Joey and Pacey pulled off their comedy routine. Even Bethany and Bruce Bowers' *Romeo and Juliet* managed to be almost touching. Sure, the show was often amateurish. Elmo and Ellen Beard couldn't sing or dance any better than they had the year before or the year before that, but their spirit and enthusiasm was unmistakable.

For a moment, Dawson felt as if he were standing outside himself, watching the show. If he could have bottled the moment, he would have. He felt quietly, deeply and totally happy. But even as he had that thought, the moment had passed. Nothing stood still or stayed the same. It was scary and sad and wonderful, all at the same time.

Capeside is your town
Capeside is my town . . .

Was it really the finale, so soon? The entire audience clapped along, as the cast sang and danced their hearts out. When they finished, the applause was thunderous. But the cast didn't take their bows. Instead, the lighting changed to a soft, amber glow, as the cast parted and one very small girl came forward.

It was Serena, her face illuminated by the flickering candle she carried in her hand. The audience hushed as Serena began to sing.

Silent night, holy night
All is calm, all is bright . . .

Dawson smiled. Serena might be a spoiled brat, but when she stopped trying so hard, she had the voice of an angel. He had wanted to end the Follies not on a boisterous note, but on a note of wonder. Serena's solo had been a secret from even the cast, until they'd rehearsed their bows just before the show.

Sleep in heavenly peace
Sleep in heavenly peace.

When Serena finished, there was a beat of utter silence. Then the audience rose to its feet, applauding, whistling, yelling "Bravo," and the cast took their bows to "Jingle Bell Rock."

Gale and Mitch hugged Dawson. "I'm so proud of you," Gale said.

"Thanks, Mom."

As people hurried over to congratulate Dawson, he searched the teeming crowd for Arthur and

Leonard, but didn't see them anywhere. Had they walked out, hated it? But the mayor had said at intermission that—

Dawson laughed out loud.

"What's so funny?" Andie asked, as they shared a hug.

"Me," Dawson replied. "I was actually worrying about whether we had impressed Arthur and Leonard, which is ludicrous. It's Capeside's show. And Capeside loved it, I think."

"Well, Dawson my friend," Pacey said, clapping Dawson on the back, "evidently so did Arthur and Leonard."

Dawson's heart hiccuped. "How could you know that?"

"Well, the subtle clue was when I overheard them just now, backstage with their newly famous wives. The fatter one—I forget which is which—said, and I quote, 'best damn family entertainment money can buy.'"

"If that's a joke, Pacey, it is decidedly unfunny."

"No joke," Pacey assured him. "Dawson Leery, Broadway's Youngest Director. It has a certain ring to it, don't you think?"

Chapter 14

It was the most incongruous smell imaginable in Capeside, Massachusetts on a Christmas Eve: hamburgers, barbecued chicken, and hot dogs cooking on a barbecue grill.

But to Dawson, it was one of the best. It had been years since his family and the Potters had done their traditional backyard Christmas Eve barbecue. He didn't know how he'd managed to convince Gale and Mitch that they should start the tradition again. Now that they were running a restaurant, he'd figured there was little chance they'd want to cook a discretionary meal for company. But to his surprise, they'd readily agreed. Maybe his success with the Follies had something to do with it. It seemed as if everyone had Christmas spirit to spare this year. In fact, his parents had even suggested that Dawson invite his friends.

Which is why they were all bundled up down by the creek, shivering, watching the sun set across the water, food sizzling on the grill, even though it was only a little after four o'clock in the afternoon. Dusk came early to Capeside in late December.

The temperature hung near freezing. No one cared.

"You pulled it off," Joey told Dawson, as they stood side-by-side, watching the sun sink below the horizon. They'd illuminated torches and placed them around Dawson's yard, so there would be plenty of light.

Dawson smiled. "We all did." He looked toward the mouth of the creek where Jen, Pacey, Andie, Bill, and Jack were starting to assemble the traditional Christmas crèche. Dawson was glad to see that Andie was speaking to Bill again. He seemed like a good guy to Dawson.

"I used to look across the creek at that nativity scene when I was in middle school, and I'd think about how lucky you were to have it," Joey confessed.

"But we'd all put it up together!" Dawson protested.

"True. But it was on your side of the creek," Joey pointed out. "And when it wasn't up, it was in a box in your garage. We didn't have one in our garage."

"Hey." Jen came over to them. "Recovered from the show, guys?"

"Mostly but not wholly," Dawson admitted. "When I fell asleep last night, I found myself dreaming that I was in the show, with Pete McCutter directing. And you know something? I was really happy."

"I heard that," Pacey said as he strolled over to them. "No show for you, Dawson. By this time next year, you will be Boy Wonder Rich and Famous Dawson Leery."

"Highly doubtful, Pacey. Regardless of what you think you overheard Leonard and Arthur say, they didn't even bother to say a word to me after the show. My conclusion is, they were saying nice things for their wives' benefit."

"You could be wrong," Jen said. "Stranger things have happened than our little show ending up on Broadway."

"Like what?" Joey asked.

No one had an answer.

They stood silently for a moment, knowing how foolish it was to hope that Arthur and Leonard would actually select Capeside's show for the production on Broadway. But you never knew, right?

Mitch Leery rang his dinner bell. "Okay, sunset's over, Merry Christmas, everyone. Come and get it before it freezes!"

There were two picnic tables set up near the house, not far from the barbecue grill. Everyone walked toward the tables; Jen's grandmother fell into step alongside Dawson.

"I just wanted to say one thing to you, Dawson, before we eat," Grams began.

"What's that?"

"This Christmas season has not been easy for my granddaughter, Jennifer. In fact, that might be the understatement of the new century. However, it would have been even less easy if not for you. I simply wanted to tell you that someone noticed. And that someone is very, very grateful." Before

Dawson could say a word in response, Grams strode away.

"Dawson, ready for some food?" his father called to him. "Directing that show must have taken a ton of energy. I'm proud of you. Your mom and I are both proud."

"Thanks, Dad," Dawson said, reaching for a paper plate. "I just thought—"

The cell phone by Mitch's grill rang, and he picked it up. "Merry Christmas," he answered. "Yes . . . Yes . . . Well, hold on one minute, I'll see if he's available. It *is* Christmas Eve, you know."

Mitch covered the mouthpiece of the phone. "Dawson, it's for you."

"Who is it?"

Mitch shrugged and held out the phone.

"This is Dawson."

"Dawson, Dawson. Arthur here!"

"And Leonard. Of Arthur and Leonard. We are so, so glad that you're there. You know who we are, right?"

Dawson could barely breathe. They really had called him. They were obviously on a speaker phone somewhere. He forced himself to control his emotions. "Of course. How are . . . Gwen and Charma?"

At the words Gwen and Charma, all of Dawson's friends instantly figured out who Dawson was talking to. They gathered around him, trying to figure out what was going on just from Dawson's half of the conversation.

"The women are fine," Leonard assured him. "We got some talented wives, eh, Dawson?"

"Yes, sir, you do."

"They do what?" Andie hissed, but Jen loudly shushed her.

"So we called to wish you a Merry Christmas, Happy Chanukah, Terrific Kwanzaa, etcetera, etcetera," Leonard quipped.

"Thank you," Dawson said. "The same to you."

"The same what?" Andie whispered, and was loudly shushed again by the group.

"We were so glad that you could spend part of the holiday season in Capeside," Dawson told them.

"It was terrific, Dawson. Just terrific," Arthur assured him jovially.

Following that, only silence came through the phone. Did he dare ask them what they thought of the show, now that they had some time to think about it?

Oh, why not, he thought. My asking them isn't going to make them change their opinion of it, or of me.

But Arthur cut him off at the pass. "I suppose you want to know what we thought of the Follies. Professionally speaking, that is."

"Yes, I would appreciate any feedback you have on the Follies," Dawson said. He glanced at Jen, who gave him a questioning look. Andie held both hands in the air with her fingers crossed for luck.

"It's a funny business, this show business," Leonard mused. "We went to scout another show today. This afternoon, actually."

"Down here not too far from New York. I have to tell you that, artistically speaking, we prefer the Capeside Winter Follies," Arthur said.

"You're kidding," Dawson blurted out. He could barely believe his ears. "You can't mean . . . are you saying you're taking the Winter Follies to Broadway? That's amazing."

All around him, his friends stood in stunned amazement. Did Dawson just say what they thought he'd said?

"I didn't say that," Leonard said quickly. "I said we preferred your show artistically. But when Arthur and I ran the numbers on the production, it was clear to us that to bring the Capeside production to New York would have been an extreme financial risk, while this other show is located close enough to New York so that we wouldn't have to pay a per diem to the actors. That means they're not on the road and we don't have to cover their expenses."

"I know what it means," Dawson said.

"And house them," Arthur added. "Show biz is a risky business. We're always trying to think of a way to minimize the risk. So when the director of this other holiday show stepped up to bat and said she'd become a major investor, why, the decision was made right then and there."

Dawson sat at the picnic table, all hope dashed. "So the bottom line is, you're not picking our show?" His eyes met the eyes of his friends, one by one, sharing their disappointment with his own.

"Kid, are you there?" Leonard called into the phone.

"I'm here," Dawson said. He swallowed hard. It had been close. Allegedly, anyway.

"We're sorry, Dawson," and Dawson heard the sincerity in Arthur's voice. "I wish we could do both shows. What you did in Capeside had heart. It did our hearts good to see it."

"Thank you," Dawson replied. "You know, it doesn't make any difference, but just out of curiosity, could you tell me what show you did pick? So I can look for it on Broadway?"

"Sure," Arthur said. "We're putting up the Christmas/Chanukah/Kwanzaa extravaganza mounted in Teaneck, New Jersey. It's funny, because the director—you know, the woman who's putting up all the cash for us—said she used to strut her stuff in Capeside. Muffy Smitham? She's got some years on her, but she's got the neck of a thirty-year-old, you can't help but notice. You know her?"

Dawson started to laugh. Then he laughed harder, and harder, so hard that his stomach hurt.

"What's so funny, Dawson?" Pacey asked. But Dawson just waved him off, wiping tears of mirth from his eyes.

"Bye, guys, thanks for calling, happy holidays," he managed to get into the phone, still laughing. He hung up and tossed the phone on the table.

"No Broadway for us, huh?" Andie deduced, obviously crestfallen.

"Sorry," Dawson said. "I do have some good news, though."

"What?" she asked.

"Pacey just won thirty dollars on his Muffy bet." His friends looked utterly confused, but Dawson figured there was time enough to explain later.

He took Joey's hand. "I'd like to sing a song about

Capeside, to the tune of 'This Land Is Your Land,' care to join in?"

"No!" everyone shouted.

Dawson laughed. "Somehow I knew that. So why don't we all sing 'Silent Night'? The way we all used to?"

"You really are a sucker for tradition, Dawson Leery," Joey murmured to him. Then she opened her mouth and began to sing.

Dawson joined in, then Grams, Andie, Jack, and finally everyone, singing in crystal clear tones that rang out in the frosty air.

"It's not snowing, Dawson," Joey whispered, her voice hushed. "But this is even better."

Dawson looked up. The first stars were out. It was a Capeside Christmas. And Joey's hand was still in his.

About the Author

C. J. Anders is a pseudonym for a well-known young adult fiction–writing couple.

Dawson's Creek: The Secret Files

It's decision time for the teens as college
approaches, and they face the fact that their lives
will change for ever. With full access to their journals,
e-mails, letters and high school yearbooks,
Dawson's Creek: The Secret Files is everything
you need to know and more, illustrated with
scores of colour photos.

Dawson's Creek: The Secret Files is available
from your local bookshop price £12.99, or simply ring
the Bookpost 24 hour orderline on 01624 844444,
postage and packing free in the UK.

A selected list of Dawson's Creek books available from Channel 4 Books

The prices shown below are correct at time of going to press. However, Channel 4 Books reserve the right to show new retail prices on covers which may differ from those previously advertised.

The Beginning of Everything Else	Jennifer Baker	£3.99
Long Hot Summer	K. S. Rodriguez	£3.99
Shifting Into Overdrive	C. J. Anders	£3.99
Major Meltdown	K. S. Rodriguez	£3.99
Double Exposure	C. J. Anders	£3.99
Trouble in Paradise	C. J. Anders	£3.99
Calm Before the Storm	Jennifer Baker	£3.99
Don't Scream	C. J. Anders	£3.99
Too Hot To Handle	C. J. Anders	£3.99
Tough Enough	C. J. Anders	£3.99
Playing For Keeps	C. J. Anders	£3.99
Running on Empty	C. J. Anders	£3.99
Capeside Christmas	C. J. Anders	£3.99
Dawson's Creek Omnibus 1	Baker/Rodriguez/Anders	£5.99
Dawson's Creek Omnibus 2	Rodriguez/Anders/Baker	£5.99
Dawson's Creek Omnibus 3	C. J. Anders	£5.99
Dawson's Creek Omnibus 4	C. J. Anders	£5.99
Dawson's Creek Official Postcard Book	None	£4.99

All Dawson's Creek titles can be ordered from your local book-shop or simply ring the Channel 4 Shop on 0870 1234 344, email shop@channel4.co.uk, fax 0208 324 5678 or fill in this form and post it to The Channel 4 Shop, 32–34 Park Royal Road, London, NW10 7LN.
Please make all cheques payable to the Channel 4 Shop.

Name ————————————————————————

Address ————————————————————————

————————————————————————————

————————————————————————————

Card Name: Visa ❑ American Express ❑ Mastercard ❑ Switch ❑ please tick one

Expiry date ———/———/———

POSTAGE AND PACKAGING FREE FOR ALL ADDRESSES IN THE UK

www.panmacmillan.com   www.channel4.com